Praise for the Book

'As an experienced practitioner of business, Partha has many stories to tell. A student of life, Partha brings forth his sharp intellect and analysis told in a simple manner. A useful handbook for most, I think this book is a must-read for the young generation of entrepreneurs that India boasts.'

—M.D. Ramesh, President & Regional Head, South & East
Africa, Olam International, author of
Amazing Africa: A Corporate Journey

'Partha demonstrated the power of entrepreneurial vision by giving up his lucrative corporate assignment and plunging whole-heartedly into developing the next cadre of empathetic business leaders. His book is a simple-to-read guide to enjoying the journey to business success and becoming a better person in the bargain.'

—Ravi Pandey, President International, Rolta, United Kingdom

'Everyone at some point has dreamt of becoming an entrepreneur. This amazing book is the ideal faithful companion for your entrepreneurial journey where you need much more than just passion for succeeding. A must-read for anyone who has an entrepreneurial dream and for those who wish to bring more entrepreneurship in their current jobs. Don't miss it!'

—Rahul Gambhir, Managing Director, Twinings Pvt Ltd, India

'In the book, Partha asks a provocative question "Why do entrepreneurs do what they do?" He threads together multiple facets of entrepreneurship to answer that question. By connecting the dots between what entrepreneurs do and who they are, Partha paves the way for a reflective entrepreneur who is self-aware and more effective. A fascinating read for every entrepreneur.'

—Dr Ankush Chopra, Professor of Strategy and Innovation, School
of Management Fribourg, Switzerland,
author of *The Dark Side of Innovation*

'*Unmet Needs of Entrepreneurship* is a refreshingly different and interesting take on the entrepreneurial journey. Partha analyses the psychology and needs that end up defining how folks handle various stages—starting from deciding to take the plunge to figuring out what works for building a business and the often unfortunate reality of failure. He adds a nice human element to the frameworks and concepts. A good read for anyone curious about the psychology of entrepreneurship and the issues and emotions involved in that journey.'

—Saumil Majmudar, Co-founder & Managing Director, Sportz Village

'Entrepreneurship is mostly a lonely journey. Partha has weaved his insights and understanding of human psychology to give new meaning to the structure of needs and its impact on various aspects of business. He provokes the reader to reflect on many aspects of entrepreneurship. The witty illustrations, simple models and numerous examples make it a highly readable book. I highly recommend it for students, budding entrepreneurs and business leaders.'

—Dr G. Shainesh, Professor of Marketing, IIM Bangalore

'Partha has brought a unique perspective to the hyper-analytical world of entrepreneurship. By turning the spotlight on the emotional drivers for the key players in the entire value chain, he has added a whole new dimension to the way one ought to look at the success drivers for entrepreneurship: a truly fresh perspective.'

—Hari Ponnekanti, Corporate Vice President and Fellow, Applied Materials Inc., California

'Whether you are a current or an aspiring entrepreneur, this is a gem of a book which takes a unique perspective to help align your purpose with your goals. Partha's twenty years of entrepreneurial experience shines through this book, and packs incisive tips, advice and useful frameworks, to help you make thoughtful and smart decisions for yourself, your family and your work.'

—Amita Choudhury, Global Diversity and Inclusion Director, Unilever

Unmet
Needs of
Entrepreneurship

S. Parthasarathy completed his MBA from IIM Bangalore in 1994, after which he joined ITC Classic and worked as a Merchant Banker. After spending two years in the financial sector that was facing challenges post various banking scams, he decided to follow his heart and started his entrepreneurial journey with very little financial resources. He ideated and executed multiple businesses over a span of two decades with a typical 'jugaad' mindset—these include a successful manpower recruitment agency, web-based apartment management solutions, and a web-based application that offered online accounting and contacts management solutions for microenterprises in India. He is also the co-founder of Magichive, a firm that is focused on the needs of parents and children.

In his spare time, Parthasarathy loves to trek, meet new people and pursue his interest in amateur astronomy. Currently, he holds the position of Head-Alumni Relations in IIMB and resides in Bangalore with his wife and two children.

Unmet Needs of Entrepreneurship

Why Entrepreneurs Do What They Do

S. PARTHASARATHY

RUPA

Published by
Rupa Publications India Pvt. Ltd 2018
7/16, Ansari Road, Daryaganj
New Delhi 110002

Sales Centres:
Allahabad Bengaluru Chennai
Hyderabad Jaipur Kathmandu
Kolkata Mumbai

ISBN: 978-81-291-5112-4

Second impression 2019

10 9 8 7 6 5 4 3 2

For
Subha, Varun and Varsha
who enrich my life

Contents

Preface

The genesis of this book lies in my first post on LinkedIn titled—'The Unmet Needs of an Entrepreneur'. I received a majorly favourable response to the perspectives highlighted in that article, and several people suggested I write a book. But I was quick to realize that writing a one-page article on LinkedIn was very different from writing a book! I decided to take up this challenge. This writing journey, based on my experience of more than two decades as an entrepreneur, began in earnest in November 2015.

The central theme of this book revolves around the idea of *needs*. Whenever I explored the idea of starting a new business, I began by asking myself, 'What are the unmet needs of the customer?' However, I realized that I never asked questions about my needs. If my needs do not get met, sustaining the motivation to work on the customer's needs is going to be a challenge. Needs play an important role as a motivating force that enables people to move into action. It impacts many areas of entrepreneurship. This book is an attempt to provide a perspective on the various needs of running a business.

I was intrigued by the work done by my wife, Subha, who runs a counselling and training centre in Bengaluru, India, that focuses on issues related to parents and children. I observed the importance of needs in understanding behaviour, and how this knowledge was being used to develop empathetic communication and a nurturing environment. I realized that the role of needs extends to the business environment: where we deal with customers, teammates, bosses, subordinates and investors. Although there are references in literature to the role of needs, it has not been given the importance that it deserves.

The book begins with the chapter 'Getting Started with Entrepreneurship', which analyses the reasons why people are reluctant to take up entrepreneurship. It also explores the attractiveness of the entrepreneurial journey, what you can learn from entrepreneurship, the brass tacks of starting a new venture, the desired characteristics of a start-up team, and the process of defining a mission and goals. You will be introduced to the iPROCESS model to help you set your goals. This chapter also explores limiting beliefs and the corresponding empowering beliefs that can help in working towards your goals.

The chapter on 'Unmet Needs of an Entrepreneur' explores the reasons for someone to get into entrepreneurship. What needs of a business are met by meeting the unmet needs of a customer? What is the main purpose of running a business? Do market conditions attract a person to take up entrepreneurship, or does the individual attract a specific kind of business opportunity? Who are you? What are needs and values? How can you discover your personal values? What is the role of the family? These and several other questions are intended to provoke the reader to reflect and dig deeper into the various fundamental aspects of entrepreneurship.

The journey to understanding customer needs starts by framing a Complete Needs Statement (CNS) and a Complete Unmet Needs Statement (CUNS). Later in the book, the ANIC model has been introduced to help the reader frame these two important statements. Together, the CNS and CUNS statements can be a useful tool in the hands of anyone working with a customer.

In the chapter, 'Customer Needs—Discovery Process and Logical Levels' the model is extended and linked to the 'neurological levels' of Dr Robert Dilts. Logical levels trace its roots to Dr Gregory Bateson's work on learning levels and further back to Bertrand Russell's work on logic and mathematics. Dilts's logical levels have been used extensively to categorize the meaning of needs, consequences, customer profiling and decision-making criteria. The ANIC model is easy to understand and lends itself to diffusion across teams in an organization.

The chapter titled 'Perceived Reality, Innovation, and New Ideas Generation' is dedicated to the need for innovation and new idea generation. The chapter focuses on *breakout innovation*, its characteristics and the skills that one can develop to generate new ideas. The reader is introduced to Tina Seelig's creativity model and the role of creativity in innovation.

Often, what we do on a daily basis is exactly opposite to what we desire in the long term. This disconnect between short-term actions and long-term needs is analysed in the chapter 'Disconnect Between Needs and Actions'. This conflict is explored through the lens of the OFNR model (Non-Violent Communication) that provides a better understanding of the underlying issues.

Entrepreneurs often face the question: 'Do I want to be a *pioneer* or a *follower*?' To bring clarity, I have analysed different decision-making patterns that people employ in the chapter 'Entrepreneurial Dilemma: Pioneer or Follower?'. This chapter explores growth, inclusiveness and the challenges of creating a motivated team. The reader is introduced to intrinsic and extrinsic motivation. The FROG model provides insights into elements that act as a catalyst to motivate you to do something.

This model highlights the role of catalysts in providing the momentum required to achieve one's goals.

The chapter 'Connectedness and Empathy' explores the role of empathy in building a nurturing, compassionate organization. How to connect to people, improve one's life and use language that is life-enriching is illustrated using Non-Violent Communication (NVC). The AAA model lays the foundation for the process of change.

Of late, emotional intelligence (EI) has started to gain prominence in business organizations. Hypothetical situations have been taken to illustrate the ABCDE model (Rational Emotive Behavioural Therapy) of Dr Albert Ellis. This model is useful in building EI in individuals and organizations. EI starts with emotional awareness. This chapter studies the relationship between emotional states and business performance. Examples illustrate reframing techniques that can help develop EI.

When businesses fail, the usual focus is on various numerical analyses. Seldom is there any focus on the personal challenges that entrepreneurs face and how they cope with failures. The last chapter, 'Coping with Business Failures', deals with the strategies that can help in overcoming these challenges at the level of beliefs, emotions and behaviour. Strategies for building resilience and an optimistic attitude are listed. This chapter highlights the behavioural signatures that impede progress.

I have illustrated many of the concepts using examples, anecdotes and cartoons. The examples quoted span the personal and professional life of an entrepreneur that highlights the application of the ideas to various contexts. Many examples are taken from the parent-child domain because of the impact of childhood on an adult's beliefs, feelings and behaviour.

Who can benefit from this book? MBA students,

entrepreneurs, marketing personnel, leaders, academicians and many others will find value in the ideas articulated in this book. The idea is to trigger the reader to think, reflect and derive meaning that is most apt for the reader's circumstances.

This book is written in a language that is simple to understand, and the masculine gender is used for convenience. Throughout the book, the masculine gender can be replaced with the feminine gender without loss of meaning.

S. Parthasarathy
4 December 2017

1

Getting Started with Entrepreneurship

'I want to but...'

I have heard many of my friends confess, 'I want to do something of my own' but they have not been able to get themselves to do it. Most of them are employed, have saved enough money to take care of family expenses, have expertise in different areas and leadership skills, can manage hundreds of people, have extensive business networks and a strong desire to do their 'own thing'. For many of them, entrepreneurship helps fulfil that desire. There is an element of glamour attached to entrepreneurship. It could also be that grass on the other side always looks greener.

Since the aspiring entrepreneurs have all the required resources to start the journey, I usually ask them 'What stops you from going on your own?' The typical responses I come across are:

'I need to save more before I can take the plunge.'
'I am not sure what I need to be doing.'
'I have expertise in so many things, but I am short on ideas about where and how to start.'
'I am looking for the right partners.'
'I have ideas, and I am confident they will work, but I am not prepared to take the risk right now.'

'What if I fail? Will I be able to get back into the industry?'
'I don't think I have it in me to become an entrepreneur.'

I soon realized that their head was blocking their heart from taking the plunge. Most of them had all the physical resources, yet it was their thinking that was creating the obstacles. It appeared that they were making up stories in their heads, sometimes exaggerated, that focused on the problems rather than on what they wanted. Entrepreneurship is about taking risks, working with uncertainty and enjoying the process. As an analogy, people are not trained to be parents, raise kids and take care of a family. At best, we can prepare ourselves for the journey. Similarly, entrepreneurship is about dealing with that lack of predictability, and this makes the process exciting, fulfilling and enriching. Popular quotes that capture the essence of this for me are 'Don't go where the path leads, rather go where there is no path and leave a trail' and 'Just do it.'

People follow certain preferred patterns of decision-making (as illustrated in Fig 1.1). While working towards a goal, there are some who focus on the goal because it is exciting and fun, while there are others who work towards a goal to avoid discomfort, pain and fear. People motivated by fear tend to focus on *what could go wrong*. This approach can be helpful in finding solutions to problems. However, the attitude that motivates entrepreneurs is *what could go right*. They prefer not to analyse too much and get paralysed into inaction. Entrepreneurs realize that the future cannot be predicted with certainty and they prefer to go with the flow. Obstacles will be dealt with, as and when they occur. They develop flexibility, can pivot and course-correct. This attitude helps them gain and maintain momentum.

It does not mean that people who focus on 'what to avoid' can't be successful entrepreneurs. As shown in Fig 1.2, some people like to move away from discomfort and pain when they want to go on their own. There are people who get into entrepreneurship to avoid poverty and misery. Others go on their own because they are unable to get a suitable job. These 'circumstantial' entrepreneurs can certainly be successful. Discomfort could motivate them to seek new ideas aggressively, work hard to move away from pain and develop an entrepreneurial mindset. However, this requires conscious efforts to change one's pattern of thinking.

Fig 1.1: Reasons for Pursuing a Goal

Are the Obstacles Real?

Some of the obstacles cited by the aspiring entrepreneurs were real, and some of them were just beliefs. If the obstacles are real, we need to ascertain if they can be overcome. If there is a dearth of skills, can the skills be acquired? If there is a shortage of money, can money be raised? If there is a lack of clarity, can an expert opinion be sought? If the efforts required to cross these obstacles are not commensurate with the return on time invested, you may or may not want to drop the idea.

On the other hand, if the obstacle stems from certain *limiting beliefs*, these beliefs need to be questioned. Are the obstacles real or just perceptions that are not backed by evidence?

Some such limiting beliefs are:

- It requires lots of money to start a business.
- A large team is required to develop a software product.
- A swanky office is required to get started.
- One should have a ground-breaking and unique idea to start a business.
- One should know all aspects of a business to start the journey.
- A large team of founders is required to start a business.

Fig 1.2: Reasons for Entrepreneurship

- One needs to be less than thirty years old to start a business.
- It is not possible for women to do business.
- People who fail at running a business will not be able to find a suitable job.

Zip Dial: The Untold Story of Product Development[1]

ZipDial enables global brands to engage with 100 per cent of their consumers. Their patent pending consumer intelligence platform drives solutions such as couponing, friend referrals, on-pack activations and more. Their clients include P&G, Disney and Colgate that have 2–5 times more unique users engaging on ZipDial than on any social network. ZipDial is based out of Bangalore and is a mobile VAS company that came into prominence with its implementation of missed calls for user verification, alerts and other use cases. Social networking giant Twitter acquired ZipDial in January 2015.

While the monetary value of the deal has not been disclosed, a report by TechCrunch mentioned that the deal had been closed between $30 to $40 million. ZipDial became Twitter's first acquisition in India. ZipDial was co-founded by Valerie Wagoner, Amiya Pathak and Sanjay Swamy.

Amiya Pathak was the head of product. What very few people know is that Amiya developed the first version of the patent pending platform, sitting in the comfort of his house with a fractured hand, over a period of four months. His intention was to get to an MVP (minimum viable product) and test if his idea worked. Amiya has an enviable academic record, with a Bachelor's degree in computer science from IIT Kanpur and an MBA from IIM Calcutta. This example breaks the belief that one requires a large team to develop a great product. Sometimes a lean team helps focus on the right problems.

---

[1]Source: Interview with ZipDial's co-founder Amiya Pathak.

You can challenge limiting beliefs by questioning causes, effects, meanings, evidences and consequences.

To question beliefs, the first step is to be *aware* of them. Many of these beliefs seem engraved in stone, and it becomes hard to accept that these are just beliefs. Some of these deep-seated beliefs seem to become truths that are seldom open for questioning.

Beliefs are judgements about relationships between two or more entities or ideas. They are usually stated as if they are true. The speaker often omits various aspects of the relationship. Linguistically, they are stated as cause-effects or complex equivalences. A complex equivalence occurs when two ideas are connected that do not relate to each other, such as A = B, where B has no actual connection to A. For example, 'she never smiles at me means that she does not like me' is effectively equating two statements i.e., '*She never smiles at me = She doesn't like me*'. An effective way of challenging beliefs is through questioning causes, effects, meanings, evidence and consequences.

You can question the limiting beliefs by asking:

- In what way are you not creative?
- What would happen if women were able to do business?
- What evidence do you have to back up your statement? Are there situations where this is not true?
- What would happen if you did not have a swanky office?
- Are there people who have been hired by employers despite having failed in their business venture?
- Lots of money to start a business? How much is 'lots'?

- What would happen if you were not an expert in all aspects of business?

What Makes Entrepreneurship So Attractive?

The act of getting into entrepreneurship is usually linked to the idea of contributing to a cause that impacts a large population of people. It connects a person to his or her core values. When the going gets tough, entrepreneurs motivate themselves by imagining the positive consequences of their actions.

Whose life are you leading anyway? The entrepreneur realizes that you live only once and you need to live it on your own terms.

There are many reasons why entrepreneurship can be very fulfilling. Here are some of them:

- Having fun doing something that you love.
- A personal sense of achievement of having given it a shot, irrespective of the success or failure of the business.
- Freedom to pursue what is close to your heart.
- Living life on your terms.
- Providing employment to others.
- Experiencing the excitement of ideating, designing, developing and executing a business idea.
- Experiencing a deep sense of ownership of what you are doing.

Learning from Entrepreneurship

Irrespective of whether a business succeeds or fails in meeting objectives, there is a lot of learning from entrepreneurship. More important than achieving the business goals is the kind of person that one becomes in the process. The *becoming* is more valuable than the *doing*.

Here are some core things to learn from entrepreneurship:

- The importance of integrity and its power to attract business and people.
- Increased accountability to oneself and others.
- Heightened awareness of relationships and networking.
- Improved communication and listening skills.
- Opportunity to become more empathetic.
- Improved ability to think through the nuts and bolts of a situation.
- Become a firm and an effective decision-maker.
- Realize that the boundaries of what one can achieve are usually grossly underestimated.
- Develop the quality of looking at the big picture.
- Develop qualities of perseverance and a never-say-die attitude.

How to Start a New Venture?

Once you know that entrepreneurship is an option that would meet your core needs, you are ready to start the journey with a confident frame of mind. What kind of business do you want to do? What are the unmet customer needs you want to fulfil? Who are your customers? What is the business opportunity? Here is a list of questions you should think through before taking the next step.

What are the Unmet Needs of the Customer?

The first step is to identify and list down the unmet needs of the customer. Talk to potential customers and try to understand the issues that are challenging them. Use all your five senses to read and listen carefully to what the customer is saying. There are times when the customer might not be able to articulate what he wants. In that case, you will have to develop your idea, build a prototype and test it on the market.

What Is Your Value Proposition? What Is Your Offering?

Do you have a solution that would get the 'job done' for the customer? What is the customer using right now to solve the problem? In what way is your solution better? What is the value that you are providing to the customer that is unique and different from existing solutions? What credibility do you have? You can also do a scan of the competition and check if there are well-entrenched competitors.

Do you have a competitive advantage that can be sustained? Are you clear about your business model and profit formula?

Who Exactly Is Your Customer?

What does he do for a living? What is the customer profile? (his profession, income, age, sex, geographic location, etc.) Do these customers have distinctive personality traits, values, attitudes, interests, or lifestyles?

Where Are They and How Will You Reach Them?

This question will make you think through the practical problems of finding your customers, at minimal cost and explore routes to reach them. What are the optimal channels to reach the customer?

What Will Make Them Buy?

How will you promote your product? Once the customer

experiences your product, how can you make the bond between the customer and your brand stronger and deeper? How can you build loyal customer relationships?

How Much Money Can You Spare for the Venture?

This question relates to *affordable loss*. In the worst case scenario, how much money will you lose if things don't work out? You can also give yourself a time frame for exploring entrepreneurship. You will need to know how to read the signs of an irretrievable failure so that you can cut losses and exit the business.

Building the Core Team for the Start-up

Once you have identified a business opportunity and are sure that you have a valuable solution, you can start thinking about building the initial set of core members and founders. It is important for the initial set of core team members to have *shared vision and values*.

Identifying People for the Start-up Team

Identifying the right co-founders perhaps is the most important step for start-up founders. I have seen schoolmates, college mates, office colleagues and strangers get together to start a business, not always successfully. People who have shared the same office or have known each other for years haven't been able to work together.

The easiest way to break up a start-up is to make the wrong hiring decisions. It takes time to build the right team, and the long-term needs of the start-up have to be kept in mind. Unfortunately, there is no quick fix formula for building the right kind of team. However, there are some important qualities to look for when building the team.

Shared Values

Functional expertise can be acquired by upgrading skills or by attending relevant training programs. However, the beliefs and core values of people do not undergo a fundamental change even over time. The embedded beliefs are usually not very explicit and can be discovered by analysing past actions. For example, thinking about a person's past integrity, motivational orientation, or work ethic could provide insights into that person's values.

Face-to-Face Meetings

Phone calls, WhatsApp messages and Skype meetings are not substitutes for face-to-face meetings. Informal meetings over a cup of coffee can provide insights into professional and personal matters that digital connection cannot. Speaking to others who have worked with the person can provide additional pointers. Ultimately, the hiring happens on a gut feeling, and no amount of analysis is likely to give you 100 per cent assurance that you have hired the right person.

Emotional Intelligence

Most start-ups go through various stages of pivoting, which require constant changes in strategy, a need for flexibility and the ability to re-orient your thinking. The start-up is likely to face many stressful moments when the going will get very tough. In such a scenario, how will the person respond? Does he blame the people or the circumstances for past failures or challenges? Does he take ownership of his role? What did he learn and how did it help him in doing things differently? These key questions relate to emotional intelligence (EI) which is very different from IQ. The emotional intelligence of team members is critical to the success of any venture.

Leadership Qualities

It is important to be clear about the kind of work culture that you want to develop in the organization. A work culture that promotes autonomy, freedom of expression, constant learning, empathy and compassion, will help in building organizations that are an extension of the universal needs of people. It is also a smart strategy to hire people who are smarter and more experienced than the founder, empower them to tap their innate potential and provide the necessary leadership to help them grow professionally and personally. Ability to work in groups is very important, and an 'I' centred approach to leadership can be detrimental to the development of a team culture in the organization. Ego is a result of low self-esteem, insecurity and the need to feel powerful and in control. It also reflects a lack of adaptability.

Long-Term versus Short-Term Needs

It is imperative that short-term needs do not require you to compromise on the long-term needs of the organization. Often, companies hire a person for an urgent, short-term requirement without adequate long-term career planning for that role. Similarly, I have seen founders invite software programmers to join the team as a co-founder to meet an immediate software requirement, without giving adequate thought to the long-term requirements of the organization. Hiring a person can be easy, but firing a person is a messy affair. It is important not to get pushed into making hasty decisions just to meet short-term needs.

It is a good idea to have a team with complementary skills. For example, if you are in the IT products space, your initial team will require a person with strong IT product design, development and implementation experience, and exposure to scalable systems. If your core product offering is technology (software), it is critical to have control over the product development process and the source code. It is not recommended to outsource the core product development and create dependencies that are outside your control.

Two other important functions are sales and strategy. Usually, the person looking after strategy takes responsibility for things like providing short and long-term direction, building business relationships, thinking through fundraising, evolving a broad corporate strategy, or coordinating the sales and product development plans. Regarding the initial operational aspects of accounting and finance, you can hire an accounting firm.

Although the responsibilities of the core team members are divided amongst themselves, it is important for this team to be jacks of all trades. Every core team member needs to be ready to double up and take responsibility for multiple functions in the organization. Since the start-up is starved for resources; team members will be expected to put their hands up, take ownership and ensure the success of the tasks undertaken. During the early days of the organization, it is critical for everyone to be *customer and sales-oriented*. It is important to listen closely to the needs of the customer as it might require the business to pivot a few times before really getting a grip on the business and the customer requirements. And the focus needs to be on sales, sales and more sales.

Defining Your Mission and Values

A mission gives you a sense of purpose that unifies your beliefs, values, actions and identity. It provides a perspective that is big, comprehensive, grand, and gives purpose and direction to one's life.

A mission statement reflects your values and guides numerous actions that are taken in the enterprise. Whether a mission is stated in explicit terms or not, you are constantly guided by your values in different areas of life, and you often choose strategies that satisfy those values. You are likely to take up different roles in life such as practising medicine, writing books, driving taxis, or teaching to meet some of your needs. For example, you might choose to take up teaching because you like to inspire children to reach their potential, or you might choose a career as an entrepreneur because you value independence and the joy of doing things others have not done before, or you might become a beautician because you want to help people feel good about themselves. A proper mission statement does not focus on the strategy used to fulfil the need but is broad enough to let you choose any number of strategies.

> 'Facebook was not originally created to be a company. It was built to accomplish a social mission—to make the world more open and connected.'
> —Mark Zuckerberg

Often, it is not necessary to define a mission. The pleasures of life will remain pleasurable even if you don't. It is not mandatory to attach everything you do to a mission. However, if you have a mission, you are bound to derive greater satisfaction in life and also a renewed *strength* from having met the purpose that you have set for yourself. A mission statement has the quality of energizing people.

For instance, the Apollo mission was announced by President John F. Kennedy many years before man managed to land on the moon, and the whole nation's scientists, technologists, researchers and academics were inspired to work on this project with single-minded devotion. Similarly, in the recent past, Mangalyaan, the low-cost, high-technology mission to Mars by India inspired the whole nation. Once 'Mission Mangalyaan' was announced a few years ago, all teams worked feverishly to achieve mission success. Scientists worked sixteen hours a day and were fully supported by their families and the employer (ISRO). On the other hand, Mother Teresa's mission in life was to provide material and emotional support to the poorest of the poor, without any conditions attached to it.

Fig 1.3: Mission in Life

A mission has the quality of inspiring groups of people to work towards a higher goal. The challenge is awe-inspiring, and it kindles the imagination of people and draws the best out of them.

To discover your mission, you can analyse your past actions and the strategies that have given you great pleasure, such as working on your hobbies, travelling, reading, watching movies, etc., and identify the values that were met through these actions. What was it about these actions and strategies that were most important to you? You need to examine past experiences that have excited you and think of future actions that will excite you even more. The values you derive from these experiences will define your personal and professional mission.

SOME MISSION STATEMENTS[2]

Applied Materials

'Applied Materials mission is to be the leading supplier of semiconductor fabrication solutions worldwide through innovation and enhancement of customer productivity with systems and service solutions.'

Avaya

'Provide the world's best communications solutions that enable businesses to excel.'

The Bank of New York

'Strive to be the acknowledged global leader and preferred partner in helping clients succeed in the world's rapidly evolving financial markets.'

Citigroup

'Our goal for Citigroup is to be the most respected global financial services company. Like any other public company, we're obligated to deliver profits and growth to our shareholders. Of equal importance is to deliver those profits and generate growth responsibly.'

Computer Sciences Corporation

CSC's mission is to use our extensive IT experience to deliver

---

[2]http://www.missionstatements.com/fortune_500_mission_statements.html

tangible business results enabling our clients in industry and government to profit from the advanced use of technology. We strive to build long-term client relationships based on mutual trust and respect.'

The Dow Chemical Company

'To constantly improve what is essential to human progress by mastering science and technology.'

Ford Motor Company

'We are a global family with a proud heritage passionately committed to providing personal mobility for people around the world.'

Harley-Davidson, Inc

'We fulfil dreams through the experience of motorcycling, by providing to motorcyclists and the general public an expanding line of motorcycles and branded products and services in selected market segments.'

IBM

'Operating a safe and secure government.'

Levi Strauss & Co.

'People love our clothes and trust our company. We will market the most appealing and widely worn casual clothing in the world. We will clothe the world.'

Microsoft

'At Microsoft, we work to help people and businesses throughout the world realize their full potential. This is our mission. Everything we do reflects this mission and the values that make it possible.'

Nike Inc

'To bring inspiration and innovation to every athlete in the world.'

Goal Setting for Your New Venture

What are your goals for your new business? How will you go about setting the goals? More fundamentally, what is a goal?

As shown in Fig 1.4, a goal is the difference between what you have and what you want. This difference is the problem that requires a solution. Goals are also referred as *desired outcomes*. When the goal is clear, one can plan the journey, become proactive, take ownership of the problem and start to move towards a solution. If you do not set and work towards your goals, you could end up working on goals that others have set for themselves.

To achieve your goal, you may be required to chunk down the process into several tasks. While executing the tasks, the goals need to be the guiding beacon. It is recommended that you do not do the tasks until the goals are clear and you are sure about how completing the task would help you achieve your goals. Problems cannot be solved unless you are clear about the desired outcome.

Goals require you to move from your present state to the desired state. During the journey, you will require resources that can help you achieve your goals. You will also have to be aware of the likely obstacles to achieving your outcomes.

You need to ask yourself the following questions before starting this journey:

- What do I want? (The goal)
- Why am I moving? (What is the purpose? What is

important about the goal?)
- How will I get there? (What are the resources required?)
- How else can I get there? (What are the choices available?)
- What if something goes wrong? (Do you have a Plan B? How do you plan to mitigate the risk?)

Fig 1.4: What Is a Goal?

If you think through the above questions, it will help you become *goal-oriented*. Goal orientation gives you control over the direction in which you wish to travel, and until you know what you want, what you do will be aimless, and the results will be random.

When you encounter a problem that needs to be solved, you can focus on the desired outcome (*outcome thinking*) or focus on the

In any situation, ask yourself—'What is it that you want?' When you observe others, ask yourself—'What is it that they truly want?' It will help you go beyond the behaviour.

problem (*problem thinking*). Problem thinking is associated with focusing on what is wrong and allocating blame and responsibility. Invariably, the focus begins to be on people and not on the problem itself. Many people get lost in the complexity of the problem, its history, costs and consequences. The focus on problems can be helpful in certain circumstances but in many other situations; it can distract you from moving forward.

The more you think about a problem the harder it is to find its solution. The word 'problem' itself evokes certain feelings of anxiety and concern.

Here are six reasons why goals are important:

- Goals provide focus.
- Well-formed goals help you measure your progress.
- It helps you avoid procrastination and makes you accountable to yourself.
- It makes you motivated and energized to work towards something.
- It helps you believe in yourself.
- Goals tell you what you truly want and help you discover yourself.

Goal Structuring: The iPROCESS Model

How can you define and articulate goals that are realistic, specific, aligned to your values and easily understood by all concerned? It is recommended that goals be written down and stuck in a place that is visible to you every day so that it gets internalized over a period. The iPROCESS model enables you to think through various aspects of your goals and structure your goals.

You can list down the five most important goals that you

have for yourself, in a way that makes it comfortable and understandable to you. There are eight important questions that you need to ask about these goals. Only when you have thought them through, will your goals be realistic, achievable and motivating.

'What you get by achieving your goals is not as important as what you become by achieving your goals.'
—Zig Ziglar

Identity: Are the goals in line with your values, with your identity and who you are as a person? If not, you need to work on reframing the goal or address the conflict between the goal and your identity.

Positive: Describe your goal in positive terms. Mention what you want and not what you do not want. All resources, efforts and time, can be directed towards accomplishing the new positive goal, and this makes it more achievable. For example, instead of 'I do not want to take up assignments where I would earn less than 25 per cent gross margins,' make your goal: 'I want to take up assignments where the gross margin is 25 per cent or more!'

Resources: What resources do you have? Put them down under the following five categories—objects, people, mentors, capabilities and money.

Ownership: Is the goal in your control? There is evidence to support the theory that one should expect to succeed to the extent that one feels in control of one's successes and failures. Not knowing the cause of one's successes and failures undermines one's motivation to work on the associated tasks. People who believe that they control their outcomes feel more confident about their competencies. For example, ask yourself if the following goals are in your control: 'I want to make my customers happy' or 'I want a rank in the first 500 of the JEE exam.' Well, these goals are perhaps not in your control. At best, you can provide the strategies that your customer can use to meet his needs, but you can't ensure that he is happy.

Instead, you could define your goal as ensuring that customer turnaround time is reduced by 50 per cent, or to provide 24/7 support to your customers. These are specific areas that are in your control and are likely to make your customers happy. Similarly, getting a rank in the top 500 in a competitive exam is a relative measure that is not in your control and could instead be rephrased as 'I want to get more than 60 per cent net score.' This goal is likely to translate into getting in the top 500, and you have a better sense of control of your goal.

Consequences: The consequences of achieving your outcome are likely to have an impact on the environment around you—on people, processes and objects. Working towards an outcome that is oblivious to the ecology can have an overall adverse impact on the desired outcome. The questions to be asked are: 'What are the wider consequences? What is the opportunity cost? Who else will be affected and in what way? How will others feel? What will you have to give up? What is good about the present situation? What is it that you want to keep?'

If your goal is to grow your sales by 200 per cent by the end of the year, it might require you to put in 12-hour working days and undertake extensive travel. The long work hours would mean you will have less family time with your kids, limited time for pursuing your hobbies and fewer moments for socializing with friends. Would you be willing to give up these things without a feeling of guilt or remorse, to achieve your goal?

Evidence: How will you know you are succeeding or have succeeded? How will you know when you are on the right track to achieving your desired outcome? You need the right feedback in the right quantity and it needs to be accurate. The goal must be demonstrable in sensory terms both to you and to others. The only way in which an outcome is going to be useful is if you can perceive and evaluate progress as you attempt to achieve it. How does the outcome look, feel and smell? The richer the description, the more you will empower your brain to create the desire to make the goal more attractive. Know how you will look, how you will feel, what you will see and hear after you have achieved the outcome.

For example, when your goal is specific such as 'increasing sales by 100 per cent in one year, getting at least two $50 million new accounts, increasing billable headcount by 500 people', it is easy to track your progress.

Specifics: Where, when and with whom? What is the context in which you wish to achieve the goal? Having goals as universal quantifiers or absolutes implies that the outcome is wanted in all contexts and for all circumstances, while in

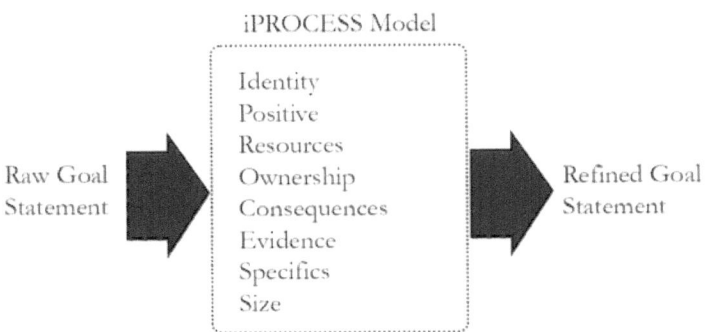

Fig 1.5: The iPROCESS Model

reality, the outcome may be useful and appropriate only in some context. For example, 'I want to be informed about every sales transaction made by the sales team on a daily basis'—do you always need all these details, or are there times when not knowing these details is acceptable and appropriate?

If you have a goal to become a writer, it will help if you are specific about the context and the time frame. Instead of stating a goal like 'I want to become a writer,' you can be more specific and change it to 'I want to write a book for teenagers in India and complete the manuscript in the next four months.' The goals need not be grandiose. If you wish to make a delectable dish for your guests, you may like to state your goals in clear terms again. Instead of 'I want to be a great cook,' state something like 'I want to make a few paneer dishes for my guests who are coming home on Sunday.'

Size: Does the goal lend itself to chunking? If the goal is overwhelming or appears to be complex and big, can you chunk it down to manageable parts? Would you be able to delegate work, if necessary, to others to accomplish parts of the tasks? If your goal is to write a novel for teenagers before the end of this year, the goal can be overwhelming. Can you chunk the writing process into manageable parts by defining things like the number of pages in one week, chapters per month, or hours of writing per day?

If you want to achieve a 100 per cent increase in sales for the next year, can you chunk the sales targets into weekly, monthly, quarterly, six-monthly targets that can be tracked and monitored closely?

What Resources Do You Have?

You should make a list of resources required to meet your goals. Broadly, these will fall into five categories, where some are more relevant than others.

Objects: You may require office equipment, a laptop, internet access, office space, software, books, CDs, videos, audio tapes, etc.

People: Could be family friends, well-wishers, acquaintances, business colleagues, and so on.

Mentors: If you are aware of someone who has already met a similar goal, it will help if you could meet this person and get some tips. If you are building a software product from scratch, you may like to talk to someone who has developed successful software products. Even if you cannot meet this person, you could read the books or articles that this person has written or follow his blog posts. Role models and mentors can help provide clarity and can add immense value to your ideas and actions.

Capabilities: Do you need to enhance some skills to meet your goal? For instance, do you need to learn programming, how to drive a car or speak a new language? You should also check if there are any personal qualities that are required to execute your goal. Are you expected to dress in a specific way? Would it require you to talk in a specific way to your customers?

Money: Do you have enough money to help you accomplish your goal? If you do not have the money, can you raise it? If you want to expand your operations, set up a factory, or buy a plant and machinery, how do you plan to fund these operations? If your goal is to buy a car, have you thought through the various funding options? If your child seeks admission to a prestigious Ivy League university in the United States and you, as a parent, do not have the necessary financial resources, are there any scholarship options for your child?

Beliefs and Goals

When your thinking about events gets reinforced over a period, the accumulated thoughts begin to harden into beliefs.

'Believe it can be done. When you believe something can be done, really believe, your mind will find the ways to do it. Believing a solution paves the way to solution.'
—David J. Schwartz

These beliefs become a reality for you, truths that seem inviolable until you make a conscious effort to question them based on new evidence. Beliefs are your best guesses at reality, but they are not facts. Beliefs give you confidence in your ideas. They shape the way you interact with the environment and with other people. They can guide you into understanding how the world works and act as permissions as well as blocks to what you can do.

The following empowering beliefs can help you in working towards your goals with confidence and energy:

- It is possible to achieve the goal.
- I have the ability to achieve this goal.
- I deserve to achieve this goal.

The three main limiting beliefs are helplessness, hopelessness and worthlessness. In other words, possibility, ability and worthiness are the three key beliefs that can help you break these limiting beliefs. Applying these three beliefs to your goals can make you aware of the obstacles to progress and take appropriate action.

Possibility: Often, we mistake possibility for skills. We think something is not possible when we do not know how to do it. Usually, we do not know our limits. You cannot know your limits until you reach them. One way to expand the world of possibilities is to tell yourself that you have not achieved the goal 'as yet'. Man landing on the moon was considered impossible at one point in time. Do not be quick to decide what is impossible.

Ability: Believing that you have not yet reached your limits helps you be open to developing the skills necessary to achieve your goals. Often, people assume they can't do something without any real evidence. There are instances of people attempting to do something a couple of times and concluding that they do not have it 'in them', based only on the small sample set of past experiences. In fact, people are usually quicker to let you know what they cannot do rather than what they can do. This focus on 'what has not been done' is all around us. For instance, at the typical parent-teacher meet at school, the teacher begins the feedback by focusing on 'where the child has lost marks', and similarly a salesman bemoans how a specific potential customer can't be converted because the salesman had made three unsuccessful attempts in the past.

Instead of exaggerating your limitations, focus on your strengths. Take responsibility for your goals and start developing capabilities that can help you in achieving these goals. When you make excuses even before the commencement of your journey, you are setting yourself up for failure.

Worthiness: Are you worthy of achieving the goals? Sometimes, people feel guilty about having more money, studying in expensive private schools, having lots of comforts, having a peaceful life, and so on. A strange thought occurs to them: 'Do I deserve these things?' This thought is a function of how you look at yourself. When you think you deserve something, the resolve and the motivation to work towards your goal is stronger. When you apply the iPROCESS model to your goals, the 'consequences' check will enable you to catch any possible moral or ethical dilemmas regarding the impact on the environment.

The Brass Tacks of Setting up a New Business (in India)

Once you have identified the core members of the new business, defined your mission, identified your values and set your goals, you need to get started on the brass tacks of starting the business.

Decide on a Name for Your Business Entity

Think of a short, catchy name. Check out the availability of the domain name. A name ending with '.in' is appropriate if your customer base is in India. If your business is going to have a global footprint in the future, then it is preferable to look for domain names ending in '.com'. If available, purchase the domain name (from a domain registrar such as GoDaddy) before even creating the business entity.

The cost of domain name registration is ₹200 (first year) and approximately ₹600+ from the second year onwards.

What Kind of a Business Entity?

You have a choice of a proprietorship firm, partnership firm, LLC and private limited company. Proprietorship firms need not be registered with any government agency. However, partnership firms in India are governed by the Indian Partnership Act, 1932, but it is not compulsory to register the firm. A private limited company has a perception of being more credible than a proprietorship or partnership firm, but is subject to many regulatory compliances. Also, it is not very easy to wind up a private limited company. An LLC is an entity that is mid-way between a partnership firm and a private limited company. You can take the advice of your chartered accountant to decide on your choice of entity.

Open a Bank Account

Banks would require entity proof and personal identity proof to open a current account. Registration under GST, Shops & Establishment Act, IEC code, MSME registration, Company registration, etc., will be accepted by banks against proof of entity. GST registration is free and can be done online. One has to visit https://gst.gov.in/ and submit all the necessary documents. If the entity being registered is a company, the bank would insist on other documents such as the list of authorized signatories, board resolutions, etc.

You can use PAN card, Aadhar card, passport, driving licence, etc., for personal identity proof. Utility bills such as electricity bill, telephone bill, water bill, etc., will be accepted for address proof.

Website and Email Creation

You can create a basic website with a few web pages and go online in less than a week (assuming you are ready with the content for it). You can hire a website designer (₹6,000 to ₹8,000 for 8–10 static pages) or design a WordPress website all by yourself. You can go for a basic WordPress hosting plan on GoDaddy and go live in a few hours' time. You can also create email boxes for free. The cost of basic WordPress hosting on GoDaddy starts at ₹99 per month and ₹199 per month on renewal. You can lock your hosting cost for the next 3–5 years if you wish. You can save a substantial amount if you take a plan for a longer duration.

Create Logo and Collaterals

Logo creation depends on your budget. You can hire professional logo designers online. You can get your logo, visiting card, letterhead and cover designs without stepping out of your home. Basic design packages cost approximately ₹8,000 to ₹10,000. Online designers can be hired from Freelancer, Fiverr, Upwork, or oDesk. You can also hire an offline designer (most printers will have designers). The cost will be around ₹500 per hour. If you are not fussy about your logo, you can design your own simple logo if you know some Adobe Photoshop basics.

Think of an attractive tagline for your business. If you have one, it needs to be included in all collaterals.

If you have a soft copy of your logo, you can visit any digital print shop and get your visiting cards designed and printed. Digital printouts are quicker, compared to screen printing, and are suited for printing lesser quantities (as low as 100 cards). Otherwise, you may have to go for screen printing where the minimum volume is much higher (500+ cards).

Cost of digital printing for visiting cards will be around ₹1.50 per card.

Accounting Systems

You will require a system to track revenues and expenses. Here are some options:

- *Manual:* You can get payment voucher and receipt voucher books printed. Ensure you get a book with a provision for a carbon copy.
- *Microsoft Excel:* Maintain details of revenues and expenses on Excel with the backup bills filed away separately.
- *Accounting software:* This would be ideal. One could

use Tally or a cloud-based solution like QuickBooks. I would recommend a cloud-based solution as it is more user-friendly. One can keep track of receivables and payables, send emails and SMS reminders. Some solutions also have a mechanism for receiving payments from customers through an integrated payment gateway.

Annual subscription cost of QuickBooks: ₹5,000+

One time cost of Tally: ₹16,000+

Mass Mailing Software

You can use MailChimp to send emails to prospective and existing customers. The advantage of MailChimp is that you can keep track of who has opened your email and view other analytics. It is user-friendly too. As you scale your operations, you can opt for paid services.

Cost: You can send 12,000 emails per month for free to a list of 2,000 email addresses.

CRM

If you need to keep track of sales leads and manage your contacts, you can look at Salesforce.com or Zoho cloud-based solutions. You can also try out SugarCRM.

The cost of SalesForce: $25 (USD) per user for five users. You can also explore other cheaper cloud-based CRM solutions.

Identify a Chartered Accountant

Auditing charges will be in the range of ₹10,000–15,000 per annum for filing IT returns and RoC filing, depending on the scope of services, nature of the entity, regulatory requirements, etc.

Summary

In this chapter, we explored reasons for people not taking up entrepreneurship despite having the desire and available resources. The obstacles were identified as being either real or just a belief. We explored the various kinds of beliefs we carry and how they limit us. Some ways to break these 'limiting beliefs' were listed.

What you can learn from entrepreneurship has been highlighted. Tips on how to start your new venture, the qualities that would help build the core team and the nuts and bolts of starting a venture have been briefly explained.

The importance of a mission was explored, and the iPROCESS model was presented to help you set goals that are realistic and achievable. We have listed the mission statements of some of the Fortune 500 companies, which will help you create one yourself.

Having a larger purpose and a set of clearly defined goals can help motivate a person get into entrepreneurship. Awareness about the nature of obstacles will provide clarity on making informed choices.

2

The Unmet Needs of an Entrepreneur

Why Get into Entrepreneurship?

In the previous chapter, we explored the reasons for people *not getting* into entrepreneurship despite seemingly having all the resources to do so. Now let us explore the reasons for people taking up entrepreneurship. When queried, the typical responses I have got from entrepreneurs are as follows:

> 'Great market opportunity and a nascent sector.'
> 'We identified an unmet need that no one was fulfilling properly.'
> 'I like the independence of doing what I want and at my pace.'
> 'If it works, it is an opportunity to make big money.'
> 'Successful entrepreneurs are more respected than professional managers. I want to be famous.'
> 'Since growth was not happening in my current job, a few like-minded friends and I got together to identify opportunities where we could leverage our experiences.'

The reasons for getting into entrepreneurship are varied. And not every venture is successful in meeting the expectations of the entrepreneur. What needs of the entrepreneur are met when he chooses to become an entrepreneur? In other words, why are you in business? These are tough questions that require introspection.

Who Attracts Whom?

Do market conditions attract a person to take up entrepreneurship, or does the individual attract a specific kind of business opportunity? We often cite reasons external to ourselves when we wish to find a rationale for doing something. Is there a characteristic in us that attracts us to opportunities of a specific kind? Will these opportunities result in success and provide us with a personal sense of alignment to who we are?

Fig 2.1: Who Attracts Whom?

Shantanu was a successful businessman. He was in the poultry business and was expanding to other markets. But something was troubling him. He did not seem happy. He said, 'I have something to share that might surprise you. Something is not right, and I get a sense that I am deceiving myself. I am living a life that does not reflect who I am.' It was startling, and on further probing, he said, 'I love pets and animals. I have kept pet dogs for more than twenty-five years, and they have given me unconditional love. It troubles me that I am doing business that involves killing animals that have reposed their trust in me for their safety.' Or take the case of Sonia, a professionally successful young lady who has strong views on feminism and gender discrimination at the workplace. She was employed by a company that made personal care products, where she was often asked to coordinate beauty pageants where female models exposed parts of their body unrelated to the product or brand image. The idea of women exposing themselves for no apparent reason made her feel very uncomfortable.

'Be yourself, not your idea of what you think somebody else's idea of yourself should be.'
—Henry David Thoreau

In both these cases, the individuals were doing something that was not in sync with who they were, and this caused discomfort and a deep sense of violation of their authentic selves. It did not meet their need for *authenticity.*

When you do something that is not aligned with who you are, you are likely to feel *uncomfortable* and *guilty of deceiving yourself.* If this guilt persists, it is unlikely that your heart will be at peace. Material success combined with a sense of being true to yourself will result in the heart being at peace. If you follow your instincts and are authentic, you will quickly realize that you begin to attract opportunities that are aligned with your true self. When this happens, your heart will no longer be at war.

As shown in Fig 2.1, irrespective of who attracts whom, when we think that we attract opportunities, it gives us a *sense of control.* It makes us accountable to ourselves. New business opportunities that are aligned with our values are likely to pop up in our head. If the opportunity is attuned to who we are, there will be a resonance between our efforts and the expected outcome, resulting in material and spiritual success.

If we assume that market opportunities attract us, there is an implicit provision for shifting the responsibility for our actions and outcomes to forces outside of ourselves to the *markets*. It gives us the option to blame the markets if something were to go wrong instead of owning up and taking responsibility.

Who Are You?

What defines you as a person? What are your core beliefs and values? Reflect back on your life and identify those activities that excited you, made you feel energized, and were highly motivating and enjoyable—activities that will not bore you even if you were to repeat them at times. Make a list of these situations. Ask yourself, 'What is it about those situations that makes me value these experiences so much?' You will start discovering the things that you value. So, what are your beliefs about what you value? You can make a list of these values and your beliefs about these values.

If you are yearning to become an entrepreneur, it is highly likely that you will unconsciously attract opportunities that are aligned with what you value. If you value the beauty of unexplored places, the wisdom of the ancient past, the togetherness of a family, the company of pets, it is likely that you will attract opportunities that are connected to these values. Some of these opportunities could be:

- Eco-tourism
- Trekking and adventure sports
- Package tours to historical places
- Pet foods business
- Pet shelters and allied services
- Organizing events for family functions
- Flower arrangements

You might get a business idea after reading a magazine, talking to your friends, or researching on the internet. In which case, you may like to check if the opportunity is aligned with your beliefs and values. If the opportunity has a high likelihood of involving actions that go against what you believe in, you may want to question the opportunity or your belief. For instance, let us assume that you value the need for ethics in business and strongly believe that *accepting or giving bribes* is unethical. If there is a business opportunity where it is required to deal with government agencies and you are reasonably certain that it is likely to involve giving bribes, you have two choices: either let go of the opportunity or question your belief. If you have evidence that it is not necessary to bribe people, you might take another look at your belief and then take the appropriate decision.

What Needs of Yours Are Being Met?

One of the first questions we ask about a business is, 'What are the unmet needs of the customer?' We seldom ask an even more basic question, 'Why do we focus on unmet customer needs?' Needs cause people to move into action. By focusing on meeting their needs, you motivate your customers to buy your product or solution.

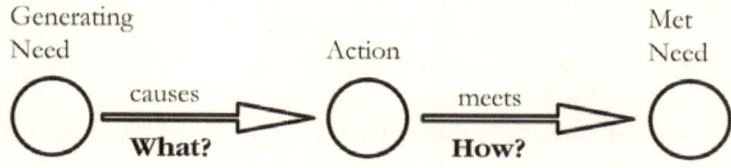

Fig 2.2: Relationship Between Needs and Action

The link between needs and action is illustrated in Fig 2.2. The *generating need* that causes people to take action does not have to be the same as the need that gets met. However, the intention of any action is to meet the generating need.

Needs are abstractions that reside as an idea in the mind-body system, and they can be interpreted differently by different people. As humans, we have identified some common principles that help us survive and lead an enriching life. All of these principles have inherent value for us. Some of these principles are directly related to the requirements of our body (for example, food, water, rest, physical well-being). However, many of our needs are ideas in mind, abstractions that can mean different things to different people. A need has two kinds of values—*inherent value* and *enhanced value*. The subjective meaning that each one of us attaches to a need determines its enhanced value. *Inherent value* derives itself from the consensus that we have about the meaning of a need that aids our survival as a species. A dictionary is a good reference point to understand the general meaning of a need. Since there is an inherent value attached to all needs,

List down your personal values. What is your interpretation of these values? What are the other possible interpretations?

these are referred to as values. This *inherent value* of a need gets *enhanced* once a context and meaning is attached to it. The importance that a person attaches to a *need* is likely to be impacted by the context and is subjective in nature. The interpretation depends on individual experiences, memories, judgements, beliefs, attitudes, and so on. People act based on their interpretations of these needs.

Here are a couple of more questions that you might like to ask yourself:

Question 1: What needs of the business are met by meeting the unmet needs of a customer?
Question 2: What needs of the entrepreneur will be met by getting into entrepreneurship?

Question 1: This question is fundamental to the existence of any business. Enterprises are in the business of providing strategies that customers can use to meet their needs. When a business provides the strategy to a customer, what needs of the business are met?

When a set of entrepreneurs come together to form a business, they do it for meeting their individual needs (see Question 2). Identifying *meaning* and *purpose* become the *core need* for the business enterprise. Purpose can mean different things to different people. Irrespective of the nature of different business enterprises, is there a universal purpose that is common to all businesses? This purpose should have the quality of motivating the workforce, and the various actions taken by the workforce will have to be geared towards meeting that purpose. Quite clearly, the common substrate for all kinds of businesses is the existence of customers and owners and the desire to serve them. These choices provoke us to ask: *Should the main purpose of a business be to meet the needs of the customers or the needs of the owners* (aka shareholders)?

Maximizing Shareholder Value

In 1973, Peter Drucker propounded that the only valid purpose of a firm is to create a customer. However, in 1976, professors Michael Jensen and Dean William Meckling published a paper that argued that the singular goal of a company should be to maximize the return to shareholders. This became very popular among corporations. During his tenure as CEO of General Electric from 1981 to 2001, Jack Welch came to be seen as the outstanding model for this theory: he grew the shareholder value at GE from a market value of $14 billion to $484 billion by the time he retired.

The real market is the world where real products and services are bought and sold, revenues are earned, expenses are paid, and real profits show up on the bottom line. The expectations market is the world where shares are traded between investors (i.e. the stock market). The stock price is determined based on *expectations* of performance.

Before 1976, professional managers were in charge of performance in the real market and were paid for performance in that real market. They were in charge of earning real profits, and they were typically paid a base salary and bonus for meeting real market performance targets.

Subsequently, CEOs and their top managers started to get paid incentives that had two components—one linked to real growth and the other linked to the value of the stocks in the expectations market, thus distracting them from the real job of running the company that produced real products and services.

It was assumed that this would improve the real performance of their companies. Studies have shown that in the period of shareholder capitalism since 1976, executive compensation exploded while corporate performance declined.

In fact, on 12 March 2009, Jack Welch gave an interview to the *Financial Times* and said, *'Shareholder value is the dumbest idea in the world.* Shareholder value is a result, not strategy. Your main constituencies are your employees, your customers, and your products. Managers and investors should not set share price increases as their overarching goal. Short-term profits should be allied with an increase in the long-term value of a company.'

Source: Roger L. Martin, 'Fixing the Game: Bubbles, Crashes, and What Capitalism Can Learn from the NFL', *Harvard Business Review Press*, 2011.

For businesses to survive, they need customers. Having more customers enhances the value for the owners and is an indicator of business growth. *If there were owners and no customers, the business would not survive.* So, to meet the basic need for survival, a business is required to focus on the customer. In other words, the purpose of every business is to *create customers and deepen relationships with existing customers.* Shareholder value is the result of meeting this need for any business.

The underlying assumption behind acquiring customers is that it will add to the *real world performance* of the business, eventually resulting in net profits. However, you are likely to notice many e-commerce companies focus on acquiring customers at such a rapid pace that profitability takes a back seat to new customer creation. Hundreds of millions of dollars are being pumped in at various stages of growth based on valuations in the *expectations world.* Every company wants to make a net profit at some point in time. The question is how long are the shareholders willing to wait? Most of these e-commerce companies are expecting value creation to happen in the world of expectations. Many funded companies have fallen by the wayside due to lack of adequate internal accruals to fund their expansion plans. Having a net positive cash flow from operations is very important for the survival of any business. *Creating new customers without due attention to the profitability in the real world is likely to create many unsustainable bubbles.*

Question 2: The second question can be reframed as 'What is it about entrepreneurship that is important to the entrepreneur?' For instance, the need for contribution or acceptance or freedom or autonomy could be the need that is met by getting into entrepreneurship. When this need is identified, it can act as an *energy booster* for an entrepreneur to work towards his goal.

People often say, 'Do what you love and your chances of being successful and happy increase.' What exactly is love? If you translate this into the language of needs and values, it essentially means, '*Do something that meets your needs and values.*'

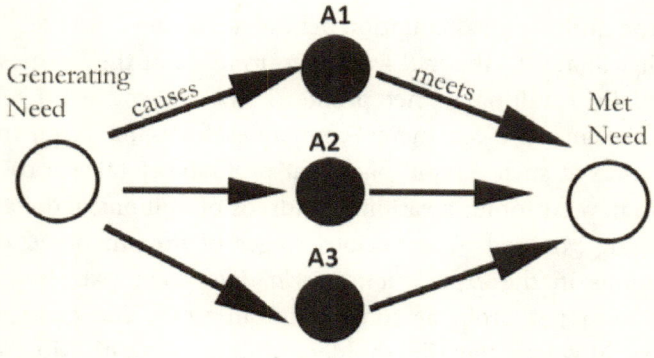

Fig 2.3: Needs as a Choice Generator

Choices to Meet These Needs

If you can identify the needs that are met by becoming an entrepreneur, it opens up a wide range of possible ways to meet that need. Needs act like a choice generator that can spew out various choices of action (see Fig 2.3). It can be used as a powerful tool to generate new alternatives.

Identifying the core need enables you to generate multiple interpretations and choices of actions with varying consequences.

These *choices of action* can be met by using multiple strategies, and each strategy will have characteristics that are distinctive vis-à-vis other strategies. Strategies refer to the specific products or services that people use to meet needs.

Akash wanted to meet his need for contribution to society by working with the underprivileged. After careful consideration of his strengths and weaknesses, along with an assessment of resources and, personal values, he decided to focus on empowering people living in remote corners of India by providing quality education at a reasonable cost.

Having identified the area of work that will help him meet his need for contribution, he had more choices to accomplish his goal. Below are some of his available choices:

- Become a teacher.
- Become a policy-maker.
- Open schools in rural areas.
- Join an NGO that is involved in teaching underprivileged children.
- Become an entrepreneur and start an e-learning business.

He had many roles to choose from. *The roles that people play are vehicles to meet their needs.* There are multiple paths to follow, and if the individual can clearly identify his needs, the path chosen will provide a sense of authenticity and satisfaction. As can be seen above, it is not necessary for Akash to become an entrepreneur to meet his needs. There are other choices available.

What Are Needs and Values?

These words are used interchangeably. All needs are valuable and what we value meets a need. As human beings, we have created a list of needs that we believe have *inherent value.* These needs enrich our lives and form the basic principles that guide our actions. These needs motivate us to act. Needs are usually described as an abstraction, such as security, safety, honesty, acceptance and structure. However, the value of these needs gets *enhanced* by giving them a meaning and a context that is subjective in nature.

Enhanced value is a subjective concept. At any point in time, some *needs* are likely to be more valuable to a person than others. The enhanced value is the result of individual beliefs and interpretations about specific needs. For example honesty could mean not taking or giving bribes. For someone else, it could mean being transparent in your dealings. Also, the value of something could change with time, both with regards the interpretation of the underlying need and with respect to its prioritization. A sample list of needs is provided in the appendix section of this book.

Role of Values

Values can guide your choice of actions. In the above example, Akash chose education as his area of work because it was aligned with something he valued dearly—equal learning opportunities for all. When what you do is aligned with what you value, your efforts are more focused, meaningful and fulfilling. Let's say he had identified low-cost housing as a way to meet his need for contribution. If that area was not in alignment with his prioritization of values, he might have entered the job half-heartedly, with a high chance of dissatisfaction (even if the business was financially successful).

How to Discover Your Personal Values?

Here are a few questions that can help you discover your personal values. Take a paper and pen, think through the following questions and jot down your thoughts:

- What would you do if you knew the world was going to end one week from today? Write down everything that comes to your mind irrespective of whether it is realistic or not. You can list down all the big dreams you have always wanted to accomplish.
- Fast forward to the end of your life. What are the three most important lessons you have learnt and why are they so important to you?
- Think of someone you deeply respect. Describe three qualities in this person that you most admire.
- Who are you at your best? List down 15–20 of your most desirable traits. Look at yourself from a third person perspective and write down those traits that characterize your true self. Do not hold back and be generous to yourself!
- What is the one-sentence epitaph you would like to be remembered for, which would capture who you were in your life?

Now that you have answered the above questions run through

them once again to filter the answers that affected you, increased your heart rate and gave you the goose bumps. Were there any commonalities between these different answers? Which answers reflect your true self?

Go through your responses to identify the real meaning behind them. If you had mentioned that 'I want to have a lot of money,' you can dig deeper to identify the core need by asking: 'What will happen if I have a lot of money?' The core need could be security or stability or to help others. Money has the quality of enabling something that you wish to fulfil and is not a value in itself.

From the filtered answers, list down 5–7 of the key values that you have identified. Cross-check if these define the real you. Are these beacons that are likely to guide the way to the life you want to lead? These are the values that truly define you. You may note that the value priorities may change over time, but some of your core values are unlikely to undergo a major change in your interpretation of them or their priority.

You can jot down these key values of yours and paste them on your desk. If you live your life by following these core values, you will find peace and congruence in all your actions. Your life might change forever!

What Needs of Yours Are NOT Being Met?

An unmet need is created when the action does not meet the generating need. The action ends up meeting some other need. As shown in Fig 2.4, this requires a change in strategy to ensure that the action meets the generating need.

As an entrepreneur, observe instances that are unsettling for you, that make you feel uncomfortable and dissatisfied. These instances are a window into your personal values and needs. When these needs of yours do not get met, they manifest as a feeling that you can experience using your five senses.

Given below are some universal needs that are highly valued by people:

- Autonomy
- Growth
- Purpose
- Competence
- Respect
- Freedom

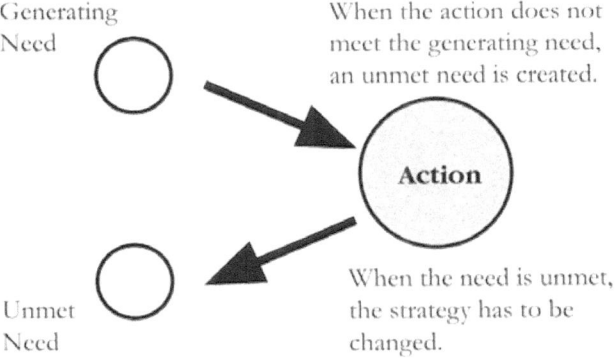

Fig 2.4: Generation of an Unmet Need

People use different strategies to meet these needs. In turn, these strategies are guided by how people interpret the needs. For example purpose for an entrepreneur could mean 'to provide primary health care and change the lives of millions of people,' whereas purpose for an employee could mean 'to have a job and provide security for family.'

When you depend on other's contributions to execute the strategies, the sense of control on the outcome is more uncertain compared to situations when the strategies are under your control.

Let us take three scenarios to illustrate the above point:

Scenario 1: An entrepreneur enters the business of providing mobile diagnostic facilities for common ailments in remote places in India. He requires the efforts of others to help him execute his strategies. If others do not give the same importance to these strategies (because their interpretation of purpose is different), it is likely that the efforts would be inadequate in fulfilling his purpose. This mismatch will ensure that his needs remain unmet, giving rise to feelings of anxiety, frustration and irritation.

A sense of ownership of the strategy used to meet a need makes you think that you are in control. It makes you feel confident and self-assured.

Scenario 2: As an entrepreneur, you value the need for autonomy. In fact, your choice of entrepreneurship was, perhaps, driven by your need for autonomy. The meaning you attach to this need is 'the freedom to make one's decisions'. It is highly likely that your employees also value autonomy. For instance, let us consider the example of designing communication material for your marketing team. Your employees have given you four different options. To exercise autonomy, you require the freedom to choose the option most suited to your requirements. Similarly, your employees would also like autonomy in designing the communication material without any interference in the design process. *Non-interference in the design process helps the designer meet his need for autonomy*. If you do not respect their interpreted need, you are likely to have employees whose needs will be unmet. If you are empathetic enough, you will be able to notice the feelings of discomfort and frustration in your employees whenever there is a clash in the interpretation of needs.

Fig 2.5: Another Interpretation of Freedom

Scenario 3: You could use yogic breathing exercises to meet your need for peace and harmony. If the strategy you use (breathing) is in your control, the likelihood of meeting your needs will be high. There is a sense of ownership of the strategy.

The above scenarios highlight the following points for an entrepreneur:

- The likelihood of strategies meeting the needs of a customer is higher when the customer has a sense of ownership of the strategy.
- People are likely to interpret the same need differently. It is important to identify the underlying needs behind

the actions of others. This understanding will help in fine-tuning one's actions so that it can help in meeting the needs of others, especially in relationships.

- Unmet needs manifest as feelings of anger, frustration, irritation, discomfort and anxiety.

Let us look at an example to illustrate the first point. When cloud-based solutions are offered to manage services such as accounting, ERP or CRM, there is initial resistance. Customers do not have a *sense of ownership* and have many issues regarding privacy of data and security. It takes time to change their perceptions about ownership, to build trust and to give them the sense of exclusive, secure ownership in the cloud. In India, Tally is the leading accounting software and is used by micro, small and medium enterprises. It is a non-cloud-based solution. Customers are reluctant to place their data on cloud-based solutions such as QuickBooks since it does not give them a sense of ownership. To sell cloud-based critical applications such as ERP and accounting requires a major change in the way customers think about ownership, privacy and security.

Businesses deal with strategies that meet customer needs. It would be helpful to:

- Become *aware* of the different strategies people use to fulfil the same needs.
- Exhibit *flexibility* to change the strategy to meet customer needs.
- Ascertain the *sense of ownership* of the strategy from a customer's perspective.
- Ensure that the *interpretation* of how a need can be met is acceptable to all involved in the execution of the strategy.

The second point highlights the impact of the differences in interpretations of needs. If you are aware of the way your employees interpret autonomy and are flexible enough to change the way you look at their interpretation, you are likely to provide space for them to meet their needs. This understanding would result in the employees being more excited to work towards meeting the shared goals of the organization.

Thinking and behavioural flexibility are important for any change to happen. Understanding the underlying need for a change will motivate you to seek the change with energy and clarity of purpose.

For example, let us assume that you have a need for punctuality that you have defined as reporting to the office on time. If your employees do not share this interpretation, it is likely to cause stress to both parties. In this case, you will have to ensure that the interpretation of punctuality becomes a shared value that is acceptable to all. Training and employee interaction sessions will ensure that both the parties are on the same page.

Need for Acceptance

Prakash is a businessman who runs five multi-location hardware stores. His wife helps him run the business. He is a first-generation entrepreneur, and it has taken him fifteen years to reach this stage, which required a lot of perseverance and hard work. Educational qualification wise, he completed a Bachelor's degree in commerce through a correspondence course. His siblings and cousins were qualified as engineers, doctors, lawyers and IT professionals. When his cousins met, they would chat about the global IT industry, mergers and acquisitions, multi-million dollar contracts, trends in HR practices, and he would invariably feel left out. When he had something to share about his business, no one seemed to understand or care. His *need to belong* was so strong that he would just hang around, laugh and shake his head as if he enjoyed being in their company. Deep in his heart, he was very uncomfortable in such gatherings. His *need for being heard and accepted* was not met.

He felt inferior and insignificant. He would think 'I am not good enough. I have not achieved anything compared to them,' or 'These guys are smart and they know so much. I must be dumb,' or 'No one cares about what I do because my work is uninteresting,' or 'I am ignored because I am not as qualified as the others.'

Prakash began to put himself down. He was low on confidence. All of us seek acceptance, from peer groups, social circles, family, friends, parents, or others. In fact, for some people, the need to be seen, to be heard and acknowledged is reflected in the number of irrelevant posts on Facebook every day, so much so that, the number of 'likes' begins to reflect the 'levels' of acceptance of the writer of the post. The lack of *unconditional acceptance* is also due to a focus on *what people do* rather than *who they are*.

> 'It is better to live your own destiny imperfectly than to live an imitation of somebody else's life with perfection.'
> —The Bhagvad Gita

Focusing on *who they are* means treating others as people and not as objects. When you look at people as people, it makes you aware that others have feelings, desires, thoughts and dreams just as you do. This unconditional acceptance forms an acceptance bridge that is not dependent on behaviour, labels and performance. The seed of the thought that 'doing something will help gain acceptance' is sown in childhood. If you observe children, you will realize that they often do things to please parents, teachers and adults who are in a position of authority. The child gets the message, either directly or indirectly, from parents and their teachers that acceptance is dependent on whether the child is good at academics, sports, arts, respectful of elders, or exhibits compliant behaviour. Unconditional acceptance requires a journey inward to help break this strong association between acceptance and behaviour.

What can Prakash do under these circumstances? Here are some options:

- Share his discomfort so that others can change their responses.
- Change himself and explore what he needs to do to belong to this group.
- Move away from the group and explore joining other professional groups where he would be unconditionally accepted.
- Work on himself, take pride in the work that he is doing, stop comparing himself to others, and develop self-respect.
- Accept that each person is unique, and that is why we are all different.

The option chosen by Prakash is likely to be one that gives him maximum satisfaction. When his chosen action meets his need, it will make him feel relaxed and comfortable.

Unmet Needs in the Personal Space: The Family

Away from the needs of the business, the unmet needs of the customer, and the unmet entrepreneurial needs, lies a very important milieu: the family. There is interdependency between one's professional and personal life. Entrepreneurs (and professionals) expect support and understanding from their immediate family.

Why Do So Many Entrepreneurs Get Divorced?[3]

The pressures on entrepreneurs and their families can take a heavy toll on relationships. There is a communication breakdown that gradually leads to incompatibility and divorce.

Common causes of divorce include financial strain, neglect, lack of communication and divergent goals. More fundamentally, people start companies to do their own things, while marriage is about doing things together. In marriages that are already strained, there is no tension a business can't make worse. Conflicting perspectives can destroy a union if the entrepreneur insists he is acting in his family's interest, but the spouse believes that he is acting on his own.

Sometimes, entrepreneurship changes a person and not for the better. In the crucible of company-building, traits such as a bossy attitude, self-importance and impatience intensify. Roger says his wife of twenty-three years dominated their relationship even before she became an entrepreneur. In his view, building a successful company made her feel so powerful and confident that she became dismissive of him. 'The seeds of our dissolution were already there,' says Roger, 'But they were like popcorn. The heat of the business made them pop up all over the place.'

Ironically, Roger says, the thrill of starting a business initially reinvigorated their relationship with freshness and energy. But over time, as his wife's workaholic behaviour continued, Roger asked if she still wanted a husband. 'She replied with some version of "Not now. Maybe later."'

Marriages are still being wrecked on the rocks of sexism: there are husbands who resent rather than celebrate

---

[3]Excerpts from www.inc.com by Meg Cadoux Hirshberg married to Gary Hirshberg, CEO of Stonyfield Yogurt.

their wives' entrepreneurial success. They could become emotionally and physically abusive in response to the spouse's growing independence.

Just as company-building can lead to divorce, a divorce can destabilize a company and even sap brand equity if the company trades on a family image. In one respect, entrepreneurs are like everyone else who divorces. They vow to do things differently next time. Many accept blame for having skewed priorities and promise their future spouses undivided attention. Underneath the grace notes of good intentions, however, the core is still intact: the business will still come first.[4]

Needs of the entrepreneur: The entrepreneur needs support (emotional and material), stability, autonomy, peace and understanding. What actions of the immediate family members would meet the needs of the entrepreneur at home? If these wants or needs are unmet, it is likely to make the affected person(s) dysfunctional:

> 'Mindfulness helps you go home to the present. And every time you go there and recognize a condition of happiness that you have, happiness comes.'
> —Thich Nhat Hanh

- When I share about events at the office, I need my family members to take interest and listen to what I have to say.
- When I come home tired from the office, I do not like to hear my kids tattling and nagging me with their

---

[4]I have listed some of the unmet needs of this interdependent relationship that are seldom discussed or given adequate importance in a business environment as it is considered outside the purview of the organization. I have assumed that the man is the sole entrepreneur at home. You can extend the logic to different scenarios at home.

sibling-related troubles, problems at school or issues with their mom, as it irritates me.

- I want my parents and my in-laws to take care of my kids and family when I need them to do so. It is challenging for my wife to do it alone.
- I do not like to listen to the problems and the constant complaints that my spouse faces at home. I expect her to deal with it.
- I want to have my personal space at home where I do not like to be disturbed.
- When I am feeling down, I expect support, encouragement and motivation from my immediate family members, not criticism and blame.
- I do not like to listen to complaints from my parents about my spouse and children. I do not like interference from elders into matters that concern my immediate family.

Needs of the Family: What are the needs of the family members? They also need support (emotional and material), stability, peace, autonomy and understanding. What actions of the entrepreneur would meet their needs? I have listed some of the possible expectations of family members:

- When our dad comes home from the office, we want him to give undivided attention to what happened at school today.
- We want our dad to spend more time with us on the weekends. Even at home or on family vacations, he is engrossed in office work, seven days a week!
- When my husband comes home, I want him to show interest and listen to what I went through during the day. I require emotional support and understanding

as well. I alone look after the needs of the kids and it is very tiring.

- When I have issues with my in-laws and discuss those with my husband, I want him to listen to my point of view and support me.
- I do not want to listen to criticisms about the cleanliness of the house, complaints about the food I make or snide remarks about home expenditure. I want financial independence.
- I want my husband to spend time on the kid's schoolwork. It is not just my responsibility to look after their material and emotional needs.
- I want my personal space and time. It is tiring to look after the needs of everyone at home.
- We (parents of the man) want our son to take us out for outings. He gives time only to his wife and kids.

The interpretation of the needs by the entrepreneur and the family members are almost the same. The difference is in the way the needs are met. Entrepreneurs need to be aware of the legitimate expectations of other members of the family. Empathy and connection are as important at home as they are in the office. If there is no appreciation and acceptance of the needs of others, it is bound to lead to unpleasantness and conflicts. There are many who have done extremely well in their professional or entrepreneurial lives but have been unhappy with their personal lives. The oft-repeated phrase 'work-life balance' is important. The challenge is about how to achieve and maintain that balance. In fact, work-life integration emphasizes the need to go beyond work-life balance and makes attempts to integrate work into one's personal life. This appreciation of balance has resulted in companies introducing flexible work hours, working from home and bringing children to a crèche at the corporate office.

When entrepreneurs focus on their needs without due importance given to the needs of people around them, it results in a disturbance in the *ecology* of the whole system. This *systemic disturbance* is likely to be detrimental to the overall health of the family system.

There are instances of people earning millions of dollars but having their family lives messed up—sometimes with children disrespecting their parents, exhibiting violent behaviour because of unaddressed emotional needs and getting addicted to drugs. At the same time, there are instances where people have not earned enough, cannot afford material wealth, but have provided unconditional love, support and comfort to their family—meeting the emotional needs of family members. Material needs of the family should not become subservient to emotional needs. People can get so engrossed in their professional lives that the unmet needs of the family often take a back seat.

What can be more painful for parents than to see their children suffer? As parents become older and wiser, they would rather trade all their wealth for the well-being of their children and for the happiness of their family. When wisdom dawns, it will be too late to turn the clock back. Connecting to the emotional needs of family members is a skill that can be acquired by attending workshops and internalizing the learnings. With regards to children, the need for parenting skills is often brushed under the carpet and parents seldom see the signs of things going wrong.

Summary

When you choose to get into entrepreneurship, it will help to think through the following important questions first:

- What needs of mine will be met? How will they be met?
- Are there other ways to meet those needs of mine?
- What are the strategies that would help me meet my needs?

I hope this chapter will also make you introspect on 'Who am I?' and make a note of the values that drive your life. We looked at examples that highlighted the need for authenticity and alignment between needs and actions. We also explored the role of values in selecting strategies that are likely to meet one's needs.

We provoked the reader to reflect on the needs that are met by a business when it meets the unmet needs of a customer, as well as the needs that are met by becoming an entrepreneur. We looked at the unmet needs of an entrepreneur, explored various choices available to meet those needs, and analysed the impact of unmet needs on people in organizations.

The last section dealt with the unmet needs of family members and entrepreneurs. This section laid emphasis on work-life balance and helping an entrepreneur become aware of his family's needs.

Needs and values play important roles in various aspects of one's life. An understanding of the manifestations and consequences of unmet needs helps in deepening your understanding of customers.

3

Perceived Reality, Innovation, and Generation of New Ideas

Most businesses are constantly looking for the next big idea that can leapfrog their earnings potential and fulfil their need for growth, creativity and innovation. So, where will these bright ideas come from? How are they going to meet their need for innovation?

During my early years of schooling, I was introduced to the concept of units place, hundreds place, thousands place (the place value system), carry over, and its application in addition and subtraction. It was a mechanical, robotic repetition of steps that we were expected to memorize and spit out when necessary. The indoctrination of the decimal number system happened soon after we stepped into class I at school.

It has now become a part of my DNA on number systems. My mind has become conditioned to think in a particular way about number systems, and for me, the decimal number system is a reality.

I would have to remove the chains that bind me to consider the possibility of other existing representational systems. Doing so is hard. Scientists did exactly that in the field of communication and computers by evolving alternate systems to meet their specific needs (Morse code, binary and hexadecimal system).

Fig 3.1: How Perceptions Shape Our Life

Let me take another example of human ingenuity and creation: the concept of money. This concept is closely tied to the number system and has become the language of economic activity. The study of economics is linked to the concept of currency and money. So much so that it impacts the way human progress and development is described and understood. It has become so ingrained in our consciousness that this artificial concept has taken over the way we think and behave. It takes conscious effort to rethink this paradigm and explore other ways of measuring and viewing human activity (barter systems, cooperative societies, qualitative growth, etc.).

The above two examples highlight the way embedded patterns of thinking substitute for reality and begin to dictate our lives. To invent something new requires breaking barriers of deeply entrenched beliefs and perceptions. In human history, breakout innovations have done just that, time and again. New idea generation requires us to break certain patterns of thinking and develop new ways of doing things. There is interdependency between the *doing* and the *thinking*. The *doing* follows the *thinking* and the *thinking* is influenced by observing the *doing*. New idea implementation requires experimentation and testing, building prototypes and showing the idea to a larger population of potential customers.

Breakout Innovation: Changing Perceived Reality

Can we, for a moment, become a Jedi and use 'the force within us' to question and change our perceived reality? When such realities are ingrained into people's consciousness, it takes quite a bit of effort to change perceptions. Just as the Jedi uses a force field that distorts the field around an object, changing perceived reality requires breaking the fabric of embedded thinking patterns. Breakout innovation goes beyond disruption; it is a revolution. It not only changes behaviour, it fundamentally changes the way one thinks.

> When something seems obvious, it takes on the quality of certainty which can limit your choices in experiencing the world. To overcome this, you need to develop self-awareness and questioning skills.

Here are a few examples of breakout innovations:

The Geocentric theory of the solar system was in vogue for at least a thousand years and was taught in all the leading universities in the world. This idea was well-entrenched in the minds of scientists, thinkers and the common man. Breaking this thinking pattern required breaking out of established patterns and unsettling the highly satisfied mind.

Darwin's theory of evolution fundamentally changed the way we looked at the evolution of life on Earth. It was revolutionary in thinking and permanently altered the way we looked at past life forms, fossils and present life forms.

The iPod is a portable media player by Apple that released in October 2001. The only comparable analog portable product was the ubiquitous Walkman from Sony. The iPod not only replaced the Walkman, but it also changed the way people began to think about portable media players. When someone thinks about portable media players, the first image they have is of the iPod and its features. The iPod is our image of how a portable media player ought to be.

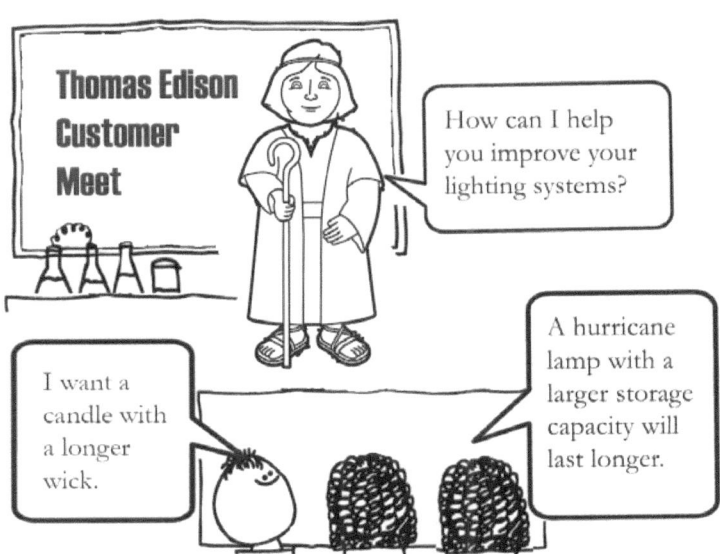

Fig 3.2: Fixed Mindsets at Work

The electric bulb changed the way people looked at lighting devices. Had Thomas Edison asked customers about how he could improve upon the existing solutions for lighting, he would have perhaps received responses such as a brighter hurricane lamp or a larger candle with longer wicks. When it comes to breakout innovations, *customers seldom know what they want*, and the solution provider is required to exhibit creativity and a flair for inventing devices that are totally different from what the customer has experienced.

> 'If I had asked people what they wanted, they would have said faster horses.'
> —Henry Ford

Facebook has revolutionized the way we think about social networks and connecting with people. The idea of connection is equated to having an active Facebook account. When we think of building relationships, we think of Facebook and other social media.

Google is so synonymous with information searches that we use it as a verb—'Have you googled it?' When we think of finding directions, the image of Google Maps pops up in our head. This image is not simply about top of the mind recall: it impacts the very way we think about directions and maps.

Uber, the transport company, has changed the way people think about taxis and personal transportation.

WhatsApp has changed the way we send short messages, share audio, videos and network with friends. It is a big leap from the SMS experience.

Breakout of innovative ideas changes our interpretation of reality and fundamentally change the way we think. It rewires our neurology and impacts the way we experience the world. It starts slowly but gains acceptance very rapidly. It is like a revolution that starts in a small way but spreads very fast.

How Do We Think?

When we experience the world using our senses, we store the observations, our interpretation of the observations, and the words that describe these observations in our memory. The words act as an anchor to the observations and interpretations and evoke certain emotions in us when we think of these stored experiences. These interpretations could be based on our direct experiences or based on the experiences of others. This interpretation can be changed if we are convinced that there are other compelling interpretations that explain a specific observation.

Each of the five senses such as touch, sight, smell, hearing and taste have certain qualities. For example, what you see can be described in detail using attributes such as brightness, contrast, whether the image is black and white or in colour, 2D or 3D, still or moving, associated or disassociated, panoramic or narrow field. Similarly, sounds can be described using attributes such as frequency, tone, rhythm, loudness, direction, mono or stereo and tempo. The sense of touch can have attributes such as location, shape, pressure, quality, intensity, movement, temperature and texture. It's the same for the other senses as well. Apparently, we store information in the form that we experience it. Language plays an important role in storing information and is referred to as a secondary representational system. We not only store information, but we are also able to analyse and categorize the information and store these associations in memory.

Words help in forming associations between various primary representational data (information received through the five senses) and their interpretations. For instance, when we hear the word dog—a quick transderivational search happens that retrieves all the associated information from memory.

In breakout innovation, a whole category of observations is replaced by a new set of observations. The qualities of the representational system (images, sounds, feelings, smells, tastes and words) undergo a fundamental change. The new idea increasingly begins to represent the whole category. Before Edison invented the electric bulb, the category of household lighting was associated with hurricane lamps and candles. The category household lighting invoked a set of images that corresponded to candles and lamps with possible variations in attributes such as the thickness, smell, or wick length. With the advent of the electric bulb, the category of household lighting evoked images of an electric bulb with variations such as size, bulb life or colour of the light. Breakout innovations alter the way one thinks about an entire category.

Breakout Innovation Characteristics

Here are some observations about breakout innovations:

- Customers are seldom able to articulate what they want.
- These wants have to be imagined by the business enterprise.
- It starts slowly but spreads very rapidly after initial acceptance.
- It has a high impact on the way people feel; it is highly exciting.
- It alters the way people think.
- People do not expect dramatic changes and are satisfied with existing solutions.
- The customers who do get attracted to the new idea

are the ones who are constantly looking for better solutions.

- There is an inherent attractiveness to the idea because it is very different from existing solutions. This quality is intrinsic, and it captures the imagination of people.
- It results in the innovation representing an entire category.

Interestingly, breakout innovative solutions do not focus on the unmet needs of the customers because *customers are not aware that there are unmet needs*. Instead, breakout innovation focuses on the needs that are met, on satisfied customers who are not looking for fundamental changes in the existing solutions. It brings about changes in the very nature of existing solutions. The customers' needs remain the same, but the strategies to meet those needs go through a fundamental change. The need for lighting remained the same, what changed was the strategy (candle or hurricane lamp or electric bulb). Breakout innovations result in the closure of most of the competitors, and it usually takes time for new competitors to start copying the new products. The competitor landscape changes rapidly.

> Breakout innovation rewires the way we think about something in a fundamental way. It replaces existing thinking with new constructs.

Incremental Innovation: Any change in existing solutions that improves customer experience and provides enhanced value results is incremental innovation. These could be existing product enhancements, improved processes, changes in the business model or a better user experience. Auto manufacturers typically make minor modifications to existing car models every two years, but without making any major changes to the vehicles. Gillette started making razors with one blade in the early 1900s. It then introduced razors with two blades, followed by three blades and now Gillette razors have as many as five blades. These are examples of incremental innovations.

In India, when you travel by train or visit local bazaars, you are likely to come across many interesting products that address specific issues that are unique and localized. Potentially, many interesting innovations are often lost or don't fit or don't get noticed or can't scale and remain in the dustbins of forgotten ideas. Even in organizations, many interesting ideas that emanate from junior or middle management executives get lost in the labyrinth of bureaucracy, organizational politics, and non-conducive work culture. The challenge is to evolve processes, practices and tools that can ensure that ideas do not get lost and the process for managing innovation is structured and consistent.

Innovation Culture in Google's Offices[5]

Google's ability to develop innovative solutions result from a number of cultural and strategic principles:

Get Everyone Involved: Google expects everyone in the company to innovate, even the administrative and finance staff. The source of the innovation matters less than the innovation itself.

Promote Creative Time: Employees are given 20 per cent of their time to pursue pet projects, unrelated to their core work, that they find interesting. Half of the new launches at Google emerged from this sanctioned time for innovation.

Encourage Volume, Speed and Iteration: Google pilots products early and often in small beta tests. This allows

---

[5]W.K. Kellogg Foundation, 'Intentional Innovation', August 2008.

people to test out ideas with others, and to iterate and refine their ideas, before launching them more broadly.

Embrace Failure: Google staffs are encouraged not to worry if an experiment in innovation fails. There is something that can be learnt or salvaged from any attempt.

The Role of Creativity

When we think of creativity, the images that are likely to arise are of people with dishevelled hair, lost in their thoughts, artistes and painters who are busy creating a world of their own or of people working in labs busy experimenting to discover something new. We are inclined to associate creativity with artistic creativity. Due to this kind of association, many people assume that they are not creative because they think they are not good at drawing, painting, music, dance, sculpting, or writing poems.

However, one can be creative while preparing a dish at home, playing a sport, writing a story, making up a song or discovering a new line of thinking in science. Creativity is about thinking new things and providing new perspectives that have not been considered earlier. It need not be about inventing something or changing the world. One can be creative even in doing small things at home. Seeing patterns that others are unable to see, connecting ideas that seem to be unrelated and discovering patterns are part of the creative process. Everybody is capable of creative achievement provided the conditions are conducive, and they have acquired the relevant knowledge and skills.

Innovation is about doing new things. The focus is on the *doing*. And to do new things, one needs to think new things. Creativity and innovation skills can be consciously developed. Developing these skills can start with the thought 'I was unaware that these skills *could* be developed,' and proceed to a stage when the application of these skills comes very naturally, almost without conscious thought. The brain gets wired to think in a certain way that promotes creativity and imagination.

It is a challenge to adhere to a structure and also ensure freedom of expression in working environments or at schools. Leaders and teachers can encourage creativity through behaviour such as:

- Asking open-ended questions.
- Tolerating ambiguity.
- Modelling creative thinking and behaviour.
- Encouraging experimentation and perseverance.
- Giving positive strokes to children or colleagues who provide fresh ideas.

Leaders, therefore, can facilitate creativity in team members. However, it is also possible to stifle creativity by being overly prescriptive, discouraging people from dreaming or having low expectations. Leaders and teachers face practical difficulties because of the pressure to focus on business or academic performance, with limited focus on efforts to encourage creative thinking.

Tina Seelig's Creativity Model

Dr Tina Seelig is the executive director of the Stanford Technology Ventures Program and the director of the National Centre for Engineering Pathways to Innovation (Epicenter) at Stanford University's School of Engineering. She teaches courses on creativity, innovation and entrepreneurship at Stanford.

Tina Seelig's creativity model enables us to understand

the various factors that impact creativity.

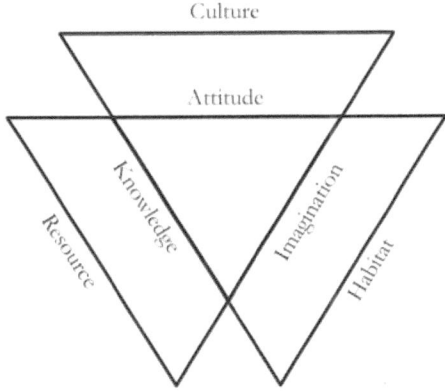

Fig 3.3: Tina Seelig's Innovation Engine

Imagination: When we think of creative people, the first phrase that comes to us is 'the power of imagination'. Some people seem to have the ability to visualize, fantasize and see patterns better than others. In fact, famous mathematicians have often said that they see numbers as pictures and images. Is the power of imagination limited to people who achieve excellence or is it a democratic characteristic that is common to all humans? The belief that it is democratic, rather than privileged, enables us to develop creativity in children and adults.

'Making the simple complicated is commonplace; making the complicated simple, awesomely simple, that's creativity.'
—Charles Mingus

Imagination is a voluntary activity that requires effort. From an ideation perspective, the challenge is how to use our imagination and thinking ability to generate new ideas.

How can we develop thinking skills to help us in the ideation process? Creativity is about seeing new patterns of associations between existing information that no one else has seen before.

Some of the skills required to generate new ideas are observation skills, divergent thinking, questioning assumptions, problem reframing, and combining and connecting ideas (association skills).

Some of the strategies used to promote thinking and creativity are playing games, deferring judgement, adding and removing constraints, forced relationships and analogies.

Knowledge: It is important to have knowledge of a specific field of study to engage in problem-solving and to make creative contributions in that field. Knowledge is a necessary but not a sufficient condition for creativity. However, it is unclear how much knowledge is necessary for creativity. Research findings are contradictory, on the one hand stating that too much expertise hinders creative outcomes, and on the other hand that there is no limit to the amount of knowledge needed to be creative. Regardless of contradictory findings, it is clear that knowledge and expertise are attributes of a creatively eminent mind.

Personality Traits: Attitudes, motivation and confidence are important personality traits that can help the cause of creativity. Also, one's beliefs and values define the kind of person that one becomes. Personal values such as wanting to make a difference in the lives of others or creating something new and unique can help the cause of creativity. Similarly, if someone has a belief such as 'a bird in the hand is worth two in the bush' or in other words is risk averse, it is likely that the person would resist moving out of his comfort zone to question the status quo. Attitude plays an important role too. For instance, a person's attitude to ambiguity can determine their willingness to explore new ideas with nebulous and uncertain outcomes. Research findings point to the importance of motivation to creativity. It has been found that intrinsic motivation fosters creativity, as opposed to extrinsic motivation (that is, motivation linked to external rewards).

Affective Processes: Emotions play an important role in creativity. The emotions that are evoked when someone is in a creative mood of discovery and exploration are excitement, exhilaration and curiosity. Our emotional responses to failures also impact our ability to persevere in pursuit of creative objectives.

The above four factors are in our control. There are also three factors that are not in our control.

Culture: Creativity depends on the social milieu that one is in—customs, norms, social behaviour, and so on. For instance, if a child is brought up in a very rigid environment where there is very little autonomy, that child is unlikely to develop creative thinking abilities. If someone's religious beliefs impose restrictions on a certain kind of thinking and behaviour, it is unlikely that the person will exercise his grey cells to think anything new that would not be accepted by the society.

Environment: The ambience of our environment also impacts the way we think. Open and airy spaces, colourful surroundings and rich sensory experiences are likely to stimulate a person to think differently. In fact, this is one of the reasons pre-schools have brightly coloured walls. Businesses invest a lot of money into making the office ambience friendly and conducive to generating creative ideas.

Resources: Access to resources such as books, computers, people and money impacts the way one thinks. The need for problem-solving through creative and original thinking is appealing when the basic needs of security, food and safety are met. To fulfil these basic needs, one requires money. However, the role of money is inconclusive. There are many instances where great creative geniuses have been born in poverty.

How to Generate New Ideas?

Generating new ideas requires us to become aware of the world around us, to question and generate alternatives. However, to implement those ideas you have to experiment and test the alternatives with a large population of people. In a world where we have developed fixed mindsets about so many things around us, is there a way we can generate new ideas by looking at things differently?

But, developing the skills below can help us in the process of generating new ideas:

- Develop Keen Awareness: Using the five senses—

Fig 3.4: Generating Ideas by Doing Things Differently

seeing, hearing, touching, smelling and tasting.

- Look for Possibilities: Questioning the status quo—How else? What else? What if?
- Explore Relatedness: Looking for patterns of relatedness using knowledge, analysis, comparisons and imagination.
- Experiment and Testing: Develop prototypes, test the hypothesis and experiment.

Developing Awareness

One can consciously develop a discerning sense of the world by sharpening observation skills using one's five senses. The ability to observe subtle nuances can help us see what others are not seeing, hear what others are not hearing and feel what others are not feeling. Observation requires noticing things the way they are, without passing judgements. Below is a set of observations that you are likely to experience on a daily basis:

Make a note of the various tasks you do on a daily basis and list down your observations without passing judgements. Check if you can generate new perspectives to the recorded observations.

- Children wear student ID cards around their neck. Some of them tend to misplace the card.
- My help at home wants to learn English. She is not in a position to afford the cost of a course.
- Parents put their children into various 'activity' classes after school hours.
- In the last two days, I have seen more than twenty senior citizens sitting and chatting for more than two hours in the park.

- I met six working couples in the last one week whose families are nuclear. The children go to daycare centres.
- I see more than five cars in the parking lot that have layers of dust.
- Our colony suffered power outage for three hours every day in the last week.
- There is a box of unused tablets in my house.
- At home, we have a crate full of unused clothes that no longer fit us.
- I see more than ten children's bicycles in the basement of our apartment complex that are gathering dust.
- The TV, the music player and the set-top box at home have different remote control devices.

When you remove the judgement part out of your observations,

> Stripping out the subjective meaning can help in experiencing something 'as it is'. The filter that we use to interpret an event can lead us to believe that there are no alternatives to a problem.

it enables you to approach a subject without any preconceived prejudices about how it needs to be done. This thinking flexibility opens up more choices for action. Some of the above observations may not be very specific. You just need to be aware of the vagueness in some of your observations. You can make observations based on your experiences or based on what others share (vicarious experiences). Indirect experiences could be from sources such as TV, newspapers, things shared by friends, social media or listening to audio recordings. Many businesses spawned because the founders faced a problem that did not have a solution in the market, for example Redbus, Johnson & Johnson (Band Aid), Housing.com, Onesolution.in, 3M Masking Tapes, etc.

My Experience with New Idea Generation

In 2008, I developed a web-based SaaS solution for the management of apartment complexes in India. It was recognized as a pioneering solution. What was the genesis of my idea? I was the first Honorary Treasurer of the owner's association of a 1,000-apartment complex. I couldn't find any software in India to manage such a large complex. The complex was one of the earliest integrated residential enclaves in India managed by an owners' association. I designed and developed a solution that was geared to meet my need for managing the complex efficiently.

In 2012, we developed another web-based SaaS solution that provided contacts management and accounting solutions for micro enterprises in India. It was integrated with an SMS and payment gateway. The idea of providing this solution emerged after observing the spouses of the founder's struggle with managing the operational aspects of their small businesses. This triggered us to talk to many similar women entrepreneurs. We did an immersion study, observed the behaviour of the entrepreneurs and spoke to them extensively to understand how they managed the operational aspects of their businesses. We noticed that most of them were either using Microsoft Excel or manual methods for bookkeeping, did not have any mechanism to track their receivables, had no reliable database of contacts, had no mechanism for reminding customers of their pending payments and had no online payment mechanism for receiving payments against bills from customers.

The above examples highlight two different methods of idea generation—one was out of one's own experience of a problem, and the other was by observing closely the challenges faced by others in solving their problems.

Looking for Possibilities: This requires questioning the status quo. It requires asking the right questions. There are two categories of questions that can help—questions that help us understand 'What is?' and questions that help us understand 'What can be?'

Asking 'Why?' can be helpful in understanding observed phenomena. It helps you analyse the causes of certain behaviour, gain a better understanding of phenomena and add to your knowledge base. The knowledge acquired by asking questions like 'Why?' and 'Why not' helps you understand the feasibility of solutions to the question 'What can be?'

However, 'Why?' is not very useful in generating new ideas. 'What else?', 'How else?' and 'What if?' are questions that can help in generating new ideas.

Let us take some of the previously mentioned observations and look for possibilities:

> *Observation*: Children wear student ID cards around their neck. They tend to misplace the cards.
> *Questions*: How else can they be identified? What else can be used instead of ID cards attached to strings around the neck? What if the card is lost? How will I identify the child?
> *Observation*: I see more than ten children's bicycles in the basement of our apartment complex gathering dust.
> *Questions*: Why are the bicycles gathering dust? What if rarely used bicycles can be sold to potential users and we take a sales commission on every transaction? How else can these bicycles be used? Can we buy and rent them to potential customers at a reasonable rate?

Exploring Relatedness: Do you see patterns of relatedness between various observed phenomena? Pattern recognition is a cognitive exercise and a *thinking skill* that can be developed. This ability requires developing *divergent thinking* and association skills that can be useful in discovering diverse choices and their interrelatedness. Discerning this relatedness requires acquired knowledge, imagination and the power to analyse, judge and compare.

Observation: Children wear student ID cards using lanyards. They tend to misplace the card.

- I have seen swimmers wear waterproof stickers. Can we have waterproof ID stickers that are part of the uniform's pocket and visible from the outside?
- I have seen names of sports players written on jerseys. Can we have the particulars of the child printed in small letters on the front pocket of the school shirt?

Observation: In the last two days, I have seen more than twenty senior citizens sitting and chatting for more than two hours in the park.

- I have seen many senior citizens wanting to share their ideas and experiences with the younger generation. Can we organize events where they can share their experiences?
- Many of them want to engage in some activity wherein they can earn some money, be financially independent and do work that is not too stressful. Are there assignments where they could work for three hours a day, have fun and earn money?
- Can we organize recreation and entertainment activities exclusively for senior citizens—where they spend time that is exclusively theirs without the presence of their children and grandchildren?

Innovations Inspired From Nature

Observing similarities between natural phenomena and human problems is an example of exploring relatedness. Here are a few innovations inspired by nature:

- The lotus leaf, due to the presence of wax, does not retain any water on its upper layer. This is called the lotus effect. Based on the lotus effect, a paint named Lotusan was developed by the German Professor Wilhelm Barthlott, from the University of Bonn. The paint is dirt- and water-repellent. It has self-cleaning properties and has excellent resistance to weather, chalk and UV rays. It remains clean for decades.

- The 500-series Shinkansen Japanese bullet train running between Tokyo and Hakata is one of the fastest trains in the world. It draws its inspiration from owl plumage to reduce air resistance, and the kingfisher's beak inspired its air-piercing nose-cone design.

- The Fast Skin Shark Suit designed by Speedo is based on the scales of a shark. The reason sharks can swim so fast is due to the design of their scales, which are covered with grooves that reduce drag by 5–10 per cent. The Fast Skin Shark Suit follows a similar design to reduce water friction and help the user swim faster.

- Velcro is the famous brand of hook-and-loop fasteners, designed by Swiss engineer George de Mestral in 1940. He designed it after observing how the hooks of plant burs stuck in the fur of his dog and his pants. Observation of the phenomena under a microscope showed him numerous tiny 'hooks' that belonged to the plant.

- Tree frogs are remarkable for their capacity to cling to smooth surfaces using large toe pads. The adhesive skin of tree frog toe pads is characterized by peg-studded hexagonal cells separated by deep channels into which mucus glands open. This enabled the frog to cling

securely to slippery surfaces. Observation of this fact has been used in designing the grooves of automobile tyres, improving the tyre's ability to grip wet roads.
- By studying how bats communicate, scientists and inventors are creating new products for the blind—including canes and sunglasses that communicate the distance to nearby objects to the user. These fascinating new tools will revolutionize how the blind interpret their surroundings and may open up new opportunities for other inventions, such as drone robots, in the future.

Experimentation and Testing New Ideas

This skill of experimentation and testing is required to be developed to ensure that the innovation is of value to the end user. After generating an idea, it is time to test its feasibility. This testing involves developing a product prototype and testing it on a sample customer base. In the IT industry, it is common practise to develop a beta version of the product that is released to a set of customers, and then the customer's feedback and suggestions are used to improve the product.

Often, test marketing is done to engage customers through informal discussions to get insights into the issues that customers are likely to face, without people knowing that they are participating in a test marketing exercise.

When we wanted to launch a web-based application for addressing online accounting, contacts management, communication and payment-based solutions for micro enterprises in India, we did an immersion study to understand customer behaviour and requirements. The study involved selling items at exhibitions and observing how women entrepreneurs handled their operations. We even opened up our prototype to a few customers to ascertain their feedback.

The study provided us with invaluable insights into fine-tuning our product.

New Idea Generation—A Study of Motor Car Rentals

When motor cars were first manufactured, they helped people travel faster from point A to point B at their convenience and on their own time. Someone noticed that it was not necessary to own a car, and there were many people who were willing to pay a small fee to travel from A to B, and thus the car rental business was born. Many variants of this model followed, based on customer needs: cars of different sizes, cars as status symbols, and service-focused offerings that enabled businesses to differentiate themselves. As technology evolved, we had taxi services that invested in hundreds of cabs to minimize the waiting time for customers. The customer would call a base station and book a cab. The operator would broadcast the requirement to all taxi cab drivers, and the person who is nearest to the customer would confirm availability and pick up the customer. Another curious person asked the question—'What if I do not have money to invest in so many cars? How else can I offer this service?' It struck him that it was not necessary to invest and own the cars. This reframing moved the business from being capital intensive to service intensive. The process of booking a cab was the same, but the cab service provider no longer owned the cars. With further advancement of technology (GPS), another inquisitive person thought—'Well, anyone who has a valid driving licence and owns a car can pick up and drop off a customer. There are thousands of cars that are grossly under-utilized. Using these cars will reduce the waiting time further.' That's how Uber was born. A host of services built around this service has made it a hugely scalable business in just a few years' time.

Every time there is a new way of doing things, it involves reframing the way one looks at something. And the good part is that these skills can be developed.

Summary

This chapter dealt with breakout innovation, perceived reality and how we can develop skills to question the status quo and generate new ideas. We introduced the idea of breakout innovations by providing examples from science and business. We made observations about the essence of such innovations and how it impacts the way we think.

We took examples of ideas that have been assumed to be true, although they are just perceptions. These ideas are so deeply ingrained in our consciousness that we are seldom aware of the fact that these are just perspectives. We have to make efforts to change our perceptions by changing the way we interpret situations.

Regarding perceived reality, the following may be noted:

- Nothing you see around you is reality. It is a perception.
- These are perspectives, and perspectives can be changed.
- You can change customer perception by changing the customer experience and their interpretation of the experience.

We listed four skills that can be developed to generate and implement new ideas:

- Develop keen awareness.
- Look for possibilities.
- Explore relatedness.
- Experiment and test.

We also provided examples of relatedness by listing innovations inspired by nature.

Generating new ideas is a skill that can be acquired through practice. However, it is not necessary to wait for a breakthrough innovative idea to get into entrepreneurship. Making incremental changes to existing solutions can be very effective in targeting niche market segments.

4

Customer Needs—Discovery Process and Logical Levels

One of the core questions that is asked before starting a business is 'What are the unmet needs of a customer?' All activities of a business are geared towards meeting this need in a way that makes the customer buy your product or service. As much as everyone knows the importance of this question, the needs discovery process is seldom clear. The challenge is, 'How to discover a customer's unmet needs?' When the underlying need of the customer is met, the customer is motivated to explore options that would make him or her purchase your offering. The solutions you offer to a customer is the strategy that the customer will use to meet his or her needs.

In this chapter, you will be introduced to powerful tools for identifying the met and unmet needs of a customer. You will learn how to construct the *complete needs statement* and the *complete unmet needs statement* using the ANIC model, and will also gain a deeper understanding of customer needs through understanding Dr Robert Dilts's work on logical levels.

What Does the Customer Need?

Many years ago, Professor Theodore Levitt had this to say about why do people buy quarter-inch drill bits: 'They don't want quarter-inch bits. They want quarter-inch holes.'

In other words, it is important to understand the *underlying needs* that provide the motivational energy for someone to take action. In this example, the drill is the strategy that is being used to fulfil a need. The relationship between needs and action is illustrated in Fig 4.1.

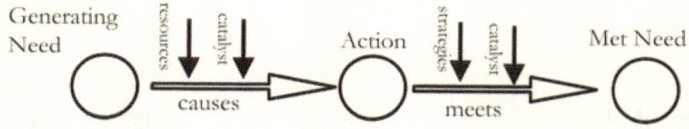

Fig 4.1: Relationship Between Needs and Action

Needs cause people to take action and addresses the question, 'What makes people move into action?' The action, in turn, is expected to meet the generating need, and it addresses the question, 'How to meet these needs?' People use different strategies to ensure that their actions can meet their needs.

Identifying the Core Needs

The discovery of needs (met or unmet) starts with the observation of an action. Behind every action is a need; or in other words, every action meets some need. Needs are not physical entities and derive their power through their interpretation in a given context.

Become aware of your various actions and the actions of others around you. Make a list of the needs that are being met and unmet through these actions. Observe the difference it makes once you become aware of the underlying needs.

Often, customers are not aware of their needs and are seldom able to articulate them clearly. In fact, we are seldom aware of our needs! The awareness of these underlying needs allows us to give different meanings to the needs, thus enriching our experiences by having more choices.

As shown in Fig 4.2, there is a need that is met by executing an action. More often than not, we are unaware of the *core need* that gets met.

Fig 4.2: There Is a Need Behind Every Action

Here are a few examples of common actions:

- The family is going for a vacation.
- A person is stealing money from the bank.
- Socializing with people despite having no common interests.
- Working for an organization.
- Visiting the temple once a week.
- Waking up early in the morning.

- Reporting to the office on time.
- Having tea early in the morning.

What needs of the person are met by doing the above actions? An action could meet multiple needs based on an individual's interpretation of the action and the need.

By asking the question 'what will the action do for you?' or 'what need of yours will be met by doing this?' you can arrive at the core need.

TABLE 4.1
Discovering Core Needs

Action	*Question*	*Meets the Need for*
Family going for a vacation	What will it do for them?	Peace, connection, fun
A person stealing money from the bank	What will it do for him?	Financial security
Hanging around with people despite having no common interests	What will it do for you?	Belongingness, acceptance
Employed with a company	What will it do for you?	Contribution, financial security, growth
Visiting the temple once a week	What will it do for you?	Peace, balance
Waking up early in the morning	What will it do for you?	Health, structure
Reporting to the office on time	What will it do for you?	Punctuality, order, respect
Having tea early in the morning	What will it do for you?	Structure, energy, health

By developing questioning skills, a salesperson can uncover a customer's core needs. For example:

> **Action:** Family going for a vacation.
> Question: What will it do for them?
> Reply: Allows them to spend quality time with each other.
> Question: What need will be met by spending quality time together? (or, what will happen if you get to spend quality time together?)
> Reply: They get to bond as a family (read it as the need for connection).

> **Action:** A person stealing money from the bank.
> Question: What will it do for him?
> Reply: He will have lots of money.
> Question: What will happen if he has lots of money?
> Reply: He will feel secure (read it as a need for financial security).

What Do These Needs Mean?

Since 'core needs' are usually stated as generalizations, they can mean different things for people. This allows people to interpret the needs based on their individual filters. The meanings are subjective in nature and can vary across individuals. These filters are based on the individual's belief systems, experiences, memories, attitudes, cultural milieu and thinking patterns.

The meaning that each one of us attaches to a need can be different based on our experiences, memories, belief systems, culture, knowledge, etc.

Identifying the meaning attached to the core need is an important step in working towards building the structure of a needs statement. The understanding of this interpretation can be helpful in providing insights into product development, market segmentation, customer profiling and product positioning.

Let us look at some interpretations:

TABLE 4.2

Different Meanings for the Same Need

Core Need	Meaning of the Need
Freedom	No cooking chores at home. Free from the pollution in the city. Having the freedom to take decisions. Participate in peaceful protests without fear of being arrested. Freedom of the press (TV, print media, the Internet, etc.). Eat food of my choice. Financial autonomy at home.
Creativity	Exploring new places. Solving math puzzles. Painting on a canvas. Get involved in sculpting. Cooking new dishes at home. Finding new solutions to problems at the workplace. Participating in theatre.
Health	Access to affordable health services. Having a six-pack and building body muscles. Appropriate body mass index. Eating vegetarian food. Free from negative thoughts. Living in a clean environment. Protection and prevention of diseases. Having organic and naturally grown vegetables, cereals, etc.

As illustrated in Table 4.2, people can have different interpretations of the same need. This insight provides clues to the way the customer thinks and how that impacts his behaviour.

Positive Consequences (or Benefits)

The next component that can help build the complete needs statement is identifying the potential consequences of an action. Actions can have negative or positive consequences. Consequences having positive implications are referred to as benefits.

Let us take a few examples to illustrate consequences. As you can see in Table 4.3, the perceived consequences of putting into action the meaning attached to a need are varied and different.

TABLE 4.3

Needs and Consequences

Need: Meaning	What are the Consequences?
Freedom: Participate in peaceful protests without fear of being arrested.	Spread awareness of the underlying cause. Open up choices and new perspectives. The government will wake up and take notice of the cause. Will build credibility for self and for the cause I am likely to become well-known and influential in society.
Freedom: No cooking, chores at home.	Enables the body to relax and rest. Find time to read books. Visit friends and socialize. Buy food from one's favourite food joint. Time to spend quality time with family. Wake up when I want to and catch up on sleep.

Freedom: Free from the noise and air pollution in the city.	Take vacations to wildlife sanctuaries and quiet places. Frequent visits to the meditation centre on the outskirts of the city. Fewer electronic gadgets at home such as high-end TV and loud music systems. Grow a home garden. Go for a trek in the mountains. Visit a village and get closer to Mother Nature. Run campaigns to increase self-awareness about pollution. Start a business in air masks to protect people from polluted air.

ANIC Model and the Complete Needs Statement (CNS)

The action-core needs-interpretation-consequences constitute the components of the *complete needs statement*. I refer to this as the ANIC model. *Interpretation* is used interchangeably with the word meaning. The CNS statement will provide insights into understanding the needs of a customer. This relationship is summarized in Fig 4.3.

> The ANIC model can help you understand behaviour, its underlying causes and its consequences that can deepen your understanding of people.

Once there is clarity on the CNS, the customer can use an appropriate strategy based on his decision-making criteria. Strategies can be from the physical or virtual world. For example, to meet the need for maintaining books of accounts (the core need is for structure which means maintaining books of accounts of transactions), a person can subscribe to an online accounting solution such as QuickBooks (virtual); to meet the need for fun and entertainment, a person can subscribe to Netflix (virtual) where the delivery and consumption of solutions happen in the virtual world or a person can purchase a two-wheeler (physical) to meet his need for flexibility and punctuality in reaching his office. The relationship between action, strategies and decision-making criteria are taken up in another section.

Customers are likely to obscure portions of their experience by using language that does not provide details. Other than the spoken language, due attention needs to be given to non-verbal communication such as body language (gesticulations, muscle movement, eye movements, facial contortions, breathing patterns, tone and pitch of voice, and rhythm). Non-verbal communication can provide insights into the way the customer thinks and feels.

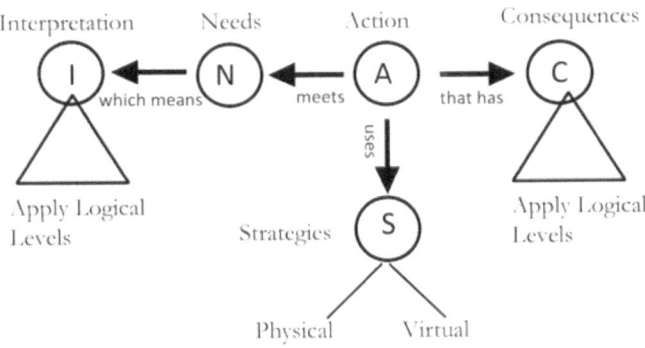

Fig 4.3: ANIC Model to Formulate CNS

Let us take an example to illustrate the process of retrieving the various components of the needs statement (these questions can be asked after building adequate rapport):

Action Statement Made by X: 'I'm late to the office today.'

Question: 'What will happen if you are late?'

X: 'I will be late for our important leadership meeting.'

Question: 'What will happen if you are late for this meeting?'

X: 'I will lose the opportunity to put forth my views and share my insightful experiences.'

Question: 'I guess you like to contribute to discussions and be heard.' (the core need for contribution, to be heard)

X: 'Absolutely. That is correct.'

Question: 'What does being heard and contributing to the discussions mean to you?'

X: 'Well, for me, a face to face interaction is more effective than drafting my views and sending it through an e-mail. It also enables me to highlight important points, take questions, share experiences and learn from the experiences of others.' (the need means face to face interactions, learning through sharing)

Question: 'What will be the consequences of being on time for the meeting so that you can contribute to the discussions and be heard by other participants?'

X: 'It helps to get noticed by the senior leadership team which can increase my chances for professional growth in the organization. I will be considered to be reliable, disciplined and trustworthy. If I am late, I could be seen as a person who does not respect other's time and that can have negative consequences.' (positive consequences—professional growth, enhance brand image)

You can retrieve lost information from an action statement by using language patterns that help you construct the different components of a need statement. You may note that consequences can also be stated as avoiding a negative consequence. In the above example, being late to an important meeting helps 'avoid an undesirable image'. You can convert the negative statement into a positive one such as 'wanting to protect an image' or 'building an image of someone who is committed and reliable.'

Logical Levels and Meaning

The idea of neurological levels, propounded by Dr Robert Dilts, is a very useful tool to deepen our understanding of needs. This model traces its history to the development of logical levels of learning by the famous anthropologist Dr Gregory Bateson and Bertrand Russell's mathematical theory of logical types.

> Logical levels refer to a hierarchy of levels of processes within an individual or group. The function of each level is to synthesize, organize and direct the interactions on the level below it. Changing something on an upper level would necessarily radiate downward, precipitating change on the lower levels. Changing something on a lower level could, but would not necessarily, affect the upper levels. These levels include (in order from highest to lowest): (1)identity, (2)beliefs and values, (3) capabilities, (4)behaviour and (5)environment. A sixth level referred to as spiritual, can be defined as a type of relational field which encompasses multiple identities, forming a sense of being a member of a larger system beyond one's individual identity.—Dr Robert Dilts

According to the Robert Dilts's model, there are six different logical levels, paralleling those defined by Bateson, that influence and shape our relationships and interactions in the world. They are shown in Fig 4.4.

One can structure one's thoughts about the meaning of a need and the consequences of an action using the logical levels. These levels correspond to the five fundamental 'W' and 'H' questions that help us organize our lives—When, Where, What, How, Why and Who. This provides a structure that can be useful in finding gaps, identifying market segments, in communication and in positioning the product.

Logical Levels and the Meaning of a Need

The meaning given to a need can be categorized under the different logical levels. What does a need mean at these different levels?

Environment: When and Where? (the external context)

Behaviour: What am I doing?

Capabilities: What am I capable of? (related to skills and abilities)

Changes at the belief and identity level impacts the levels below, viz. capability, behaviour and environment.

Beliefs: What are my beliefs about this? Why is it so important for me?

Identity: Who am I?

Spiritual: What will be the impact on the system and everyone around me?

Let us take an example to illustrate the point:

How can we categorize *freedom of movement* (the meaning attached to the need for freedom) according to the logical levels?

Environment: The law of the land allows me to travel to any place in India.

Behaviour: I like to travel by motorcycle and visit different places.

Capabilities: I have the ability and necessary skills to ride a bike.

Belief: Riding a bike symbolizes freedom.

Identity: I am a free person, and I enjoy freedom in any form.

Spiritual: All bikers and travellers love freedom.

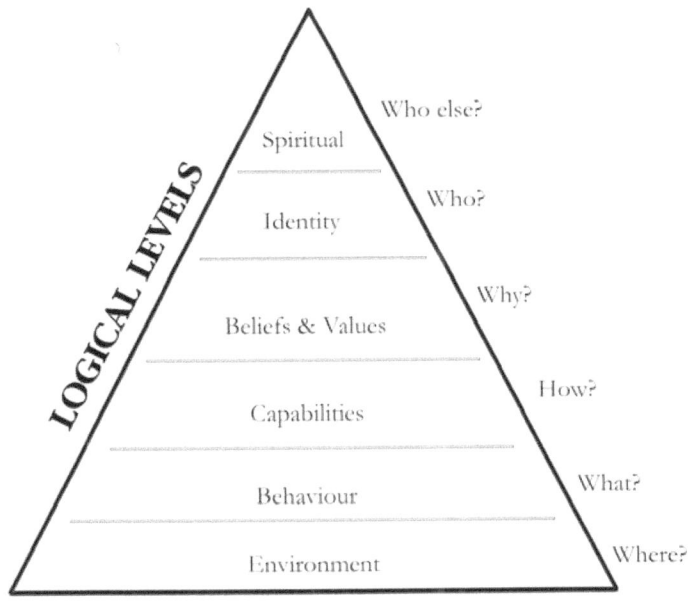

Fig 4.4: Robert Dilts's Logical Levels

How is the above information useful? Let us take the example of a company exploring opportunities for offering a bike to people who like to travel long distances. The marketing team interviewed people who travelled extensively by road, train and air. After using the questioning skills for discovering needs, they realized that extensive travel met the customer need for freedom. Freedom meant the *option to travel to any place at any time*. Although many of them enjoyed going to different places and meeting people, they appeared to enjoy the journey more than the destination.

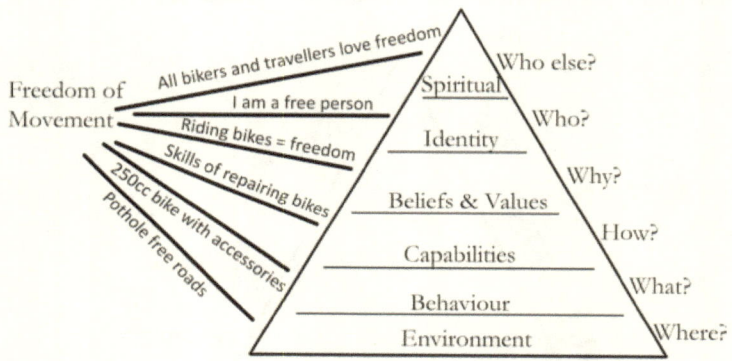

Fig 4.5 : Connecting the Meaning of Needs with the Logical Levels

The marketing team decided to dig deeper into the meanings mapped to the various logical levels (refer to Fig 4.5). Given below are some of the insights derived out of understanding these meanings:

Environment: The environment level refers to factors outside of oneself. Freedom at this level could mean freedom to move on roads without fear of accidents due to potholes or poor lighting, to have unrestricted access to remote places and to have hassle-free registration of new bikes with regulatory bodies. This finding could help the company create methods to provide all necessary help in obtaining driving licences and new bike registrations, to develop bikes that have excellent shock absorbers or make road-gripping tyres that are anti-slip with a long life.

Behaviour: Freedom could also be associated with riding a bike with a cylinder displacement of over 250cc with all the necessary accessories required for long rides. This interpretation of freedom could provide insights into the importance of power, acceleration, stability, balance, fuel tank capacity, seating comfort, accessory provisions and safety mechanisms.

Capability: If most of the customers equate freedom with minimal bike maintenance and self-sufficiency in basic bike maintenance, this might point to providing value-added training services on bike maintenance and a focus on bike design to minimize repair issues. Training programs could involve offering free classes to all customers covering basic repair, tips on different riding conditions, use of accessories in emergency situations and standard operating procedures during an emergency.

Belief: At the belief level, the discovery that most customers believed that riding a bike was an *expression of freedom* could be useful in targeting communication. Advertisements could focus on the idea of freedom and effectively equate freedom with riding a bike. This involves changing the meaning of a need.

Identity: By questioning customers on what freedom of movement meant for them, the marketing team quickly realized that a majority of customers associated freedom of movement with being a free and liberated person. This finding directly addresses the identity level and could be an important insight into understanding the customer. Communication that highlighted the connection between the action and the customer's identity would be a powerful way to motivate the customer to purchase the product.

Spiritual: When the majority of customers have a strong commonality at the spiritual level, they are likely to identify themselves as being part of a higher good, and it might be a good idea to promote biker groups that share that spirit of freedom with other like-minded people. Communication could highlight this aspect of the relationship of the biker to the strong need for belonging to a larger group with shared interests.

Logical Levels and Consequences

Dilts's logical levels can also be used to categorize positive consequences (or benefits) according to the logical levels. The benefits are closely linked to the action and the meaning attached to the need. Some benefits could be common across different interpretations of the need.

Logical level meaning and consequences of needs can be useful in segmenting markets, positioning, customer profiling and fine-tuning product offerings.

Let us illustrate through an example:

Consequences of Action and the Meaning of a Need Mapped to the Logical Levels: Let us take the previous example and categorize the positive consequences according to the logical levels.

What are the positive consequences (or benefits) of travelling by a bike to meet the need for freedom of movement?

External Environment: To explore remote places which can be accessed only on bikes, publish travelogues and become a trusted guide, start a business on guided bike tours to remote places (What are the benefits based on 'where and when' one can ride a bike?)

Behaviour: To reach destinations quickly and safely riding a bike, to easily park the vehicle, to have better control and balance at high speeds, to travel long distances, develop a deeper understanding of people and their cultures, and visit tough terrains such as mountains and deserts (What are the benefits of riding the bike?).

Capabilities: To learn bike maintenance that can be helpful when one is stuck in remote places, learn emergency skills that can be put to use to help others in distress, save money on repairs through self-maintenance, acquire skills that can be helpful when learning to drive a car (What are the benefits of learning the skills to ride a bike?).

Belief: To develop additional reinforcing beliefs such as 'long bike rides will make a person independent in thought and action,' 'people who travel widely have a rich, interesting and varied life narrative that is positive and empathetic,' 'nature must be preserved at all costs,' and 'there is beauty in everything around us' (What is the impact of riding a bike on one's belief systems?).

Identity: To develop self-esteem and self-belief that reinforces the identity of being a free and liberated person, to help others develop self-worth by becoming a role model, to begin to see oneself as a compassionate and caring person, to deepen relationships with others because of a better appreciation of the world around oneself (What are the benefits at the identity level?).

Spiritual: To spread the message of unity in diversity, develop communities that are cooperative, compassionate and empathetic, promote peace among societies, go for bike rides that promote important causes (What are the benefits to others around you?).

One way to identify benefits is to look at various situations where the action is likely to result in positive consequences. Often, companies highlight situations and the associated benefits that would accrue from using a product or a service. Customers relate to benefits easily as they are often linked to a usage context.

It is not necessary to have a meaning or a consequence mapped into all the logical levels. Customers can associate their needs to a meaning or a consequence at some levels and not to others. It is not necessary to force fit something into a logical level. The categorization can help in providing insights into the basis of any action.

How can this understanding help a marketing executive? Let us illustrate with an example:

Complete Needs Statement (CNS): The act of presenting a bouquet of flowers meets the need for love which means doing something without any conditions attached, and this results in the receiver identifying herself as being worthy of love.

The statement above highlights the action, the core need, its interpretation and its positive consequence. In this case, the benefit has an impact at the identity level of Dilts's logical levels.

This insight can highlight the identity level benefits of the product or service in marketing campaigns. Identity level benefits are a preferred space to occupy for any brand because they have a powerful impact on buying behaviour and can override product drawbacks at the lower levels.

CNS: The act of enrolling oneself in a driving school meets the need for independence which means not having to depend on my husband to travel to nearby places, and this result in boosting my self-confidence in my ability to learn new skills.

In the above statement, the benefit focuses on the belief level of Dilts's model. This new found self-confidence in being able to learn new skills easily can be transferred to the identity level in an advertising campaign. The easily learnable skills of riding the specific brand of the bike can be linked to the identity level of becoming a self-confident person, with a positive impact on other areas of life.

The process of formulating the CNS can throw up unique insights into requirements that can stem from satisfied customers whose needs are met.

Going Beyond Behaviour: Benefits of Identifying the Needs

Raghu is a salesman who has the additional responsibility of identifying trends in the market and reporting interesting insights on customer behaviour. He works for a company that just invented a smart device to control water usage in toilet commodes. The device automatically assesses the water that is required for flushing, thus saving precious water. However, they are facing adoption challenges. In the monthly sales meeting, each sales person shares his findings with the team. Raghu did not have anything to report for the meeting, but since there was peer pressure to share an experience, he shared the following:

'I visited a 600-apartments complex today, but the security guards at the gate did not allow me inside the campus,' he remarked dryly.

'Did you talk to the owners' association?' quipped Alex, a colleague.

'This is a two-year-old complex, and they do not have an owners' association because of pending issues between the owners and the builders,' replied Raghu.

'Is there any other way we could get in touch with the residents?' asked Harish, the sales manager.

'I am not able to think of anything right now. For sure, the apartment complex has an active residents' community,' remarked Raghu.

'How do you know that?' asked Harish.

'I heard a small group of women talking about waste

segregation,' replied Raghu, 'they seemed to be some part of a volunteer group.'

'That is interesting. What do you think the women were in need of?' queried Harish.

'I guess they want to use the organic compost for the common garden. This group would also be able to generate revenues by selling the excess compost,' replied Raghu.

'I think they are looking at ways to comply with the recent government guidelines to adopt waste segregation practices for apartment complexes. However, this is going to be implemented only after a year,' added Alex.

'Which need of theirs will be met by generating compost for the common garden and what needs of theirs will be met by complying with a government guideline that is non-mandatory?' questioned Harish.

'I guess it meets their need for *contribution to society*,' replied Raghu with a sparkle in his eye.

'Exactly. The volunteers were meeting their need to contribute. And one of the ways to contribute is to segregate waste. There are other ways to contribute too. How about conserving water?' asked Harish.

'I get what you are saying. If we could engage this group of women to take up the issue of water conservation, it would meet our need of providing solutions to conserve water, and it would meet their need for contributing to a cause,' remarked an excited Raghu.

The above example illustrates the importance of understanding underlying needs and interpreting them in alternative ways so that different actions can meet the same need. Raghu can offer solutions for water conservation to the women that would meet their need for contribution at the spiritual level of Dilts' logical levels.

Exercise: Can you generate a CNS for the following actions?

- Online booking of bus tickets through Redbus.
- Hiring a cab through Uber.
- Having roadside food.
- Going for an Ayurvedic massage.
- Using the laundromat services down the street.
- Purchasing organic vegetables and foodstuffs.
- Using a lending library to borrow books (for example Justbooks).
- Hiring pest control services for your apartment.

Discovering Unmet Needs

The focus of the earlier sections has been on identifying *met needs* and formulating the complete needs statement. However, entrepreneurs and marketing professionals are interested in the *unmet needs* of a customer. How do we uncover the unmet needs of the customer? Uncovering the customer's unmet needs helps us identify gaps and develop strategies to meet that need. It helps us focus on the problems being faced by the customer.

Sensory acuity helps in observing consumer behaviour and identifying a met and unmet need. Digging deeper to understand the underlying thoughts and emotions can help in understanding how the consumer thinks.

An action can do one of three things. It can meet a set of needs. It can fail to meet a set of needs. Or it can fail to meet some aspect of the customers' interpretation of an already met need.

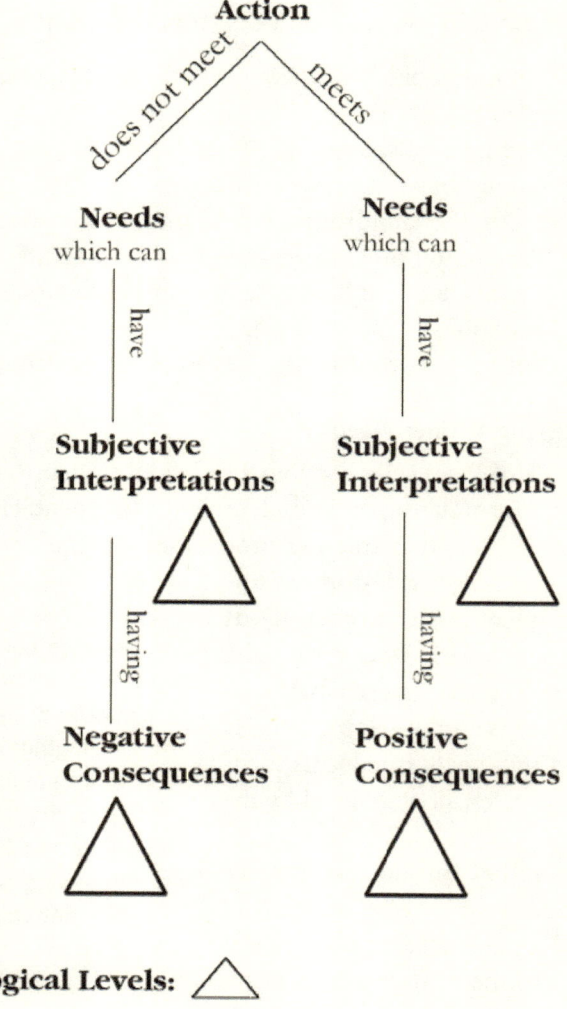

Fig 4.6: *Met and Unmet Needs of an Action*

As shown in Fig 4.6, when we analyse the unmet needs of an action, the focus is on retrieving complete information on the unmet needs by formulating a *complete unmet needs statement* (CUNS). The CUNS provides insights into unmet needs. However, the questions that need to be asked to uncover the various components of CUNS are different from those that were used to formulate the CNS.

Sensory acuity helps in observing consumer behaviour and identifying a met and unmet need. Digging deeper to understand the underlying thoughts and emotions can help in understanding how the consumer thinks.

While formulating the CUNS, the focus is on the negative consequences. This helps in understanding the problems being faced by customers and how these problems impact them.

When an action does not meet a need, questions regarding evidence procedures (How do you know that?) can be useful in gathering more information about the challenge being faced. Questions such as 'what if?' and 'how else?' can help in retrieving more information about various components of the underlying need.

The Role of Feelings

How can we know when the underlying need is not meeting an action? Non-verbal communication plays a key factor in providing the necessary cues. When a need is not met, it manifests itself as unresourceful feelings and behaviour. While some people are likely to verbalize their feelings, when a person has challenges using a product or service, you will most likely see this in non-verbal expressions. Feelings of frustration, annoyance, anger, agitation, sadness and stress, are usually associated with unmet needs and are likely to manifest themselves physiologically (i.e. facial expressions, muscle tensions, body stiffness and sweat). The art of observing these signs can be cultivated through practice and by developing sensory acuity.

Let us take some examples to help us formulate the complete unmet needs statement.

Action

A person is struggling to open the lid of a jam bottle.

Signs of a Need Not Being Met: Feelings of frustration and irritation visible by observing facial expressions, verbalized frustration through exclamations such as 'Ah! Oh!'

To discover the underlying unmet need, one would have to ask appropriate questions such as 'what exactly is bothering you?'. There could be multiple needs that are not met. It is possible that the same need is met and not met in some way, for example, you could have a product that is convenient to use in some context and not very convenient in some other context. Table 4.4 illustrates the questions that can be asked to identify the unmet needs.

TABLE 4.4
Identifying Unmet Needs

Action	Question	Response
A person struggling to open the lid of a jam bottle.	What exactly is bothering you?	It is too tight.
	What will happen if it is too tight?	Takes a long time to open and hurts my wrist.

	How would you like this changed?	It needs to be convenient and easy to open even for a child. The bottle is made of glass, and it is dangerous. I would prefer a material that is safer to use.
	Is there anything else you would like to change?	There are no clear instructions on how to open the lid.

In the above example, the needs that are not met are *convenience, safety* and *clarity*. The questioning process also provides insight into the meaning attached to these needs.

Logical Levels and the Meaning of Unmet Needs

What do convenience, safety and clarity mean in this context? The meaning is summarized below:

Meaning: Easy to open for a seven-year-old child, use of material that does not cause harm, clarity of instructions on how to open the lid.

The person is likely to respond in ways that can be mapped into the different logical levels as shown below:

Environment: 'The bottle cap is very tight. There are no instructions on the bottle. The bottle is made of glass and can cause harm.'
Behaviour: 'I am putting in too much effort, and my wrist hurts. Let me ask my spouse for help.'
Capability: 'I do not have the skills necessary to open

the lid.'
Belief and Values: 'Products of similar design are not user-friendly.'
Identity: 'I must be dumb since I do not know how to open it.'
Spiritual: 'There must be others facing similar challenges. Let me share my experiences on social media.'

If the meaning of the unmet need has an impact on the identity level, it is likely to have a negative consequence for the brand image of the product. The customer will spread the 'bad word of mouth' to others as it does not make him or her feel good about himself or herself. If the majority of customers have an issue with the skills required, the company will have to rethink the bottle lid design. Even if the instructions are clearly mentioned, and a child or a senior citizen faces problems in opening the lid, it could result in acute frustration and bad mouthing of the product.

Logical Levels and the Negative Consequences of Unmet Needs

When the needs are not met there are negative consequences, and a study of these consequences will provide insights into the challenges faced by customers. We can begin to construct the complete unmet need statement (CUNS) that captures the action-unmet need-interpretation as given below:

Action-unmet need-interpretation: 'My not being able to open the bottle lid does not meet my need for convenience. Convenience means that anyone above five years of age should be able to open it with minimum effort and the negative consequences of not being able to open it are _____.'

The blank in the above statement would capture the negative

LOGICAL LEVELS	Spiritual	I need to post this on social media so that others can learn from my experience.
	Identity	I must be dumb that I do not know how to open it.
	Beliefs & Values	Product is not user-friendly, it is perhaps not a product worth buying.
	Capabilities	I do not have the skills necessary to open the lid.
	Behaviour	I am putting in too much effort and my wrist hurts. Let me take the help of my husband to open it.
	Environment	The bottle cap is very tight. There are no instructions on the bottle.

Fig 4.7: The Meaning of Unmet Needs Mapped to Logical Levels

consequences of the unmet need. Based on interactions with customers struggling with the bottle lid, the possible negative consequences mapped onto the logical levels are listed below:

Environment: My old parents staying with me complain about the bottle lid; my medical bill expenses have increased due to frequent visits to the doctor; children hurt their hands as the bottle slipped from their hands and the glass broke.

Behaviour: I end up spending more time opening the lid; my spouse is upset with me as I ask for his help every time; I get angry with myself and with others around me.

Capability: I feel embarrassed that I do not have the skills to open the bottle lid. I am not confident in my own abilities and I am no longer interested in buying bottles with this design.

Beliefs and Values: Companies that design such products do not care for their customers.

Identity: I will not associate myself with this company and its products; I will not identify myself with such poor design.

Spiritual: Others need to be warned, I need to spread the word around. I will post my experience and thoughts on my blog.

NEGATIVE CONSEQUENCES & LOGICAL LEVELS

Spiritual	Others need to be warned. I need to spread the word around on social media.
Identity	I will not associate myself with this company and its products; I will not identify myself with this brand.
Beliefs & Values	Companies that design such products do not care for their customers.
Capabilities	I feel embarrassed that I do not have the skills to open the bottle lid.
Behaviour	I end up spending more time opening the lid; my spouse is upset with me; I am angry at myself.
Environment	My medical expenses have increased; My elderly parents complain about the lid.

Fig 4.8: Negative Consequences and Logical Levels

When the negative consequences map onto the higher logical levels, it will begin to impact the image of the company. At the behaviour level, the worst case scenario is that the customer will not buy the product. If most customers think that they have a deficiency of skills, the company can take initiatives to provide clear instructions on the process to open such lids. If the customer begins to form beliefs based on the experience, he might not want to associate himself with the company, and he could begin to refuse to purchase the company's other products. If the customer begins to believe that it is his responsibility to share this experience with other potential customers, this would relate directly to the spiritual level and can have an adverse impact on the company's image. Maximum damage can happen if the negative consequences happen at the belief, identity and spiritual level, where it could potentially impact the brand image of the product and the company.

The overall impact of the negative consequences is likely to result in losing existing customers and a potential loss of goodwill. It is said that feelings are contagious. Unresourceful customer feelings are likely to result in adverse behaviour that will propagate to others. The negative consequences mapped into logical levels are illustrated in Fig 4.8.

Complete Unmet Need Statement (CUNS)

Based on the study of the unmet needs, we can uncover the complete unmet needs statement, providing insights into the unmet needs and identifying opportunities.

CUNS: 'My not being able to open the bottle lid does not meet my need for convenience, which means that children and senior citizens should be able to open it with minimum effort and the negative consequences of not being able to open it is that I will not buy the product because the company does not care for its customers.'

The above negative consequence can be traced back to the belief level. Solving this problem will require working on the product design, as well as addressing the beliefs being formed about the company.

Given below are a couple of more examples of CUNS statements.

CUNS: 'My visit to the therapy centre for an Ayurveda massage treatment did not meet my need for cleanliness which means that the surroundings and accessories need to be spic and span. When this does not happen, I will report the matter to the management for a refund.'

(This is an environment level problem which can quickly be sorted out before the customer begins to form negative beliefs about the product or service.)

CUNS: 'The introductory talk made by the IIT exam coaching centre at the school did not meet my need for excellence in coaching. For me, this means being articulate and clear when communicating ideas. All coaching centres are money spinners who are not committed to excellence in teaching.'

(This an example of a negative consequence at the belief level.)

A CNS can help in positioning the product, understanding the met needs and exploring how the customer's experience can be improved. CUNS can be useful in identifying problems being faced by the customer, understanding customer requirements, and mitigating issues faced by existing customers. A customer will be happy to articulate his requirements and problems when his needs are not met and he is dissatisfied with existing solutions.

Exercise: Can you generate a CUNS in the following situations?

- Frequent disconnection of the broadband service.
- A patient made to wait for an hour despite having an appointment with the doctor.
- You are caught in a traffic jam.
- A colleague frequently comes late to meetings.

- You are unhappy with your existing job.
- You are irritated when you see children's clothes, school bag and school shoes lying on the floor.
- You are annoyed with the lack of appreciation for efforts that you put in at the office.
- You are upset that your employer asked you to travel to the United States at a very short notice.

Customer Value Proposition: The CVP can be developed once the CNS and CUNS have been formulated. These statements would provide you with insights into the met and unmet needs, their meanings and consequences. While formulating the CVP, other factors such as competitor offerings and existing industry structure, need to be considered to come up with a compelling, unique and differentiable offering that customers will value.

Strategy-Action Relationship

Understanding the generating need requires us to ask the question, 'What causes the action?' The next step is to understand how the action meets the needs. The action is expected to meet the generating need, but it is likely that the need being met is not the generating need. 'How to meet needs?' revolves around the domain of strategies available to meet the needs. This process involves searching, shortlisting and selecting an appropriate strategy to meet the need. Once the customer has chosen to take action to meet his or her needs, the next step is to search and apply the appropriate strategy to help meet the needs. Strategy refers to

To execute an action, you are likely to choose an appropriate strategy from among numerous options available. Strategies are the products or solutions that you use to execute an action.

the various products or services that are available to a customer. In Fig 4.9, the strategy pool refers to the numerous choices available to the customer.

To choose a strategy, the customer applies his Decision-Making Criteria (DMC), consciously or unconsciously, to the various options available. If the chosen strategy meets the needs of the customer, he is likely to be a satisfied customer. If the needs do not get met, feelings of dissatisfaction and discomfort will set in; that will make the customer evaluate alternate strategies. If the customer exhausts all the alternative strategies, he has the option of looking for alternative actions to meet his needs.

For example, if the customer has a need for punctuality, which means reporting on time to the office, he has multiple choices of actions available to him. His travel choices include taking an auto, travelling by bike or a car, taking a bus, moving to a place nearer the office or joining a car pool. Let us assume that the customer decides to select the action of using public transport to reach the office on time. This action is likely to meet the need for punctuality. However, it may not meet the need for flexibility and convenience, giving rise to a feeling of dissatisfaction. If the feelings are strong and important enough, the customer is likely to change the course of action and explore travelling by bike. If the customer chooses to travel by bike, he has multiple choices of strategies such as Honda, Suzuki, Yamaha, Bajaj, Royal Enfield, etc. These constitute the set of alternate strategies that forms the strategy pool. DMC refers to the criteria that the customer is likely to use to evaluate and select a strategy.

Understanding how the customer makes the decision to choose a strategy results in the purchase of the product or service. Dilts's logical levels can provide interesting insights

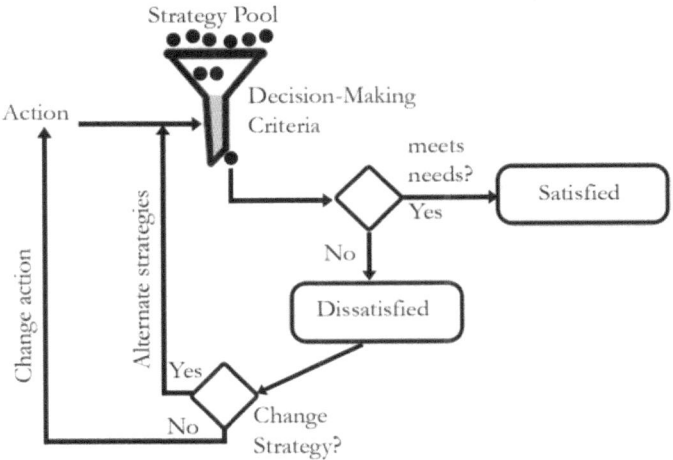

Fig 4.9: Relationship Between Strategy and Action

into the DMC of a customer.

Decision-Making Criteria: These criteria can be mapped onto the logical levels as shown below:

Environment: Product features, pricing, accessibility, ambience, etc. These factors are outside the control of the customer. The questions that the customer is likely to ask are 'What are the product features and specs? Where can I get it? When will I get it? What are its functionalities?' This level is the first stage of product differentiation.

Behaviour: This level relates to criteria that are mapped to actions, 'What can I do with this product? How will it solve my problem? What is the evidence that it can solve the problem? How efficient is the product or solution in solving the problem?'

Capabilities: The questions that the customer is likely to ask are: How easy is it for me to use the product (usability and complexity)? Do I require any special skills to use the product? Can these skills be acquired? What if I can't learn these skills?

Beliefs & Values: This revolves around important questions such as: What are my beliefs and expectations about the suitability of the specific strategy to meet my requirements? Do I believe that the chosen line of action will be able to meet my needs? Do I believe I can execute a particular line of action? What are my beliefs about the company or the organization that is providing the strategy? Do my personal values map onto the values of the strategy provider?

People feel comfortable purchasing products of Apple, Tata, IBM, etc., because they believe that these companies are trustworthy and reliable. Customers identify themselves with the values that these companies represent, and the sense of shared values has a huge impact on the purchase decision.

Identity: At this level, the customer can make decisions based on how closely he associates himself with the brand image and its values. His decision revolves around the question: 'What does choosing this strategy do to my identity?' For example, if I drive a BMW car, I will be known as a successful businessman. If I buy products from CRY, I am a compassionate and kind person. When I buy Apple products, I see myself as someone who likes quality and seeks perfection. The purchase has an impact at the identity level.

Spiritual: When a customer thinks that he is contributing to a bigger cause that goes beyond him, he is operating at the spiritual level. For example, when I buy products that have zero carbon footprint, I am contributing in lowering pollution levels and in closing up the hole in the ozone layer. When I use WhatsApp messaging service, I am contributing to the idea of a highly connected world that breaks barriers of distance, class, race and religion. When I purchase Tata Nano, I am contributing to the growth of home-grown companies.

As you can see, customers use DMC that straddle various logical levels. The larger the influence of the strategy at higher levels (belief or identity or spiritual), the higher the likelihood of the customer buying your product or service.

The higher logical levels deal with the way the customer thinks. Communication, advertising, promotion and positioning are exercises that operate at these levels.

Customer Profiling

As shown in Fig 4.10, the logical levels can be a useful tool to understand the customer.

The logical levels can help in profiling the customer. To illustrate, let us consider profiling the customer of a spirits and beverages company.

Environment: This refers to the context in which the action takes place. The context is where these customers meet their needs. The contexts could be parties, social gatherings or pubs.

Behaviour and Capabilities: You can identify the customer by his or her behaviour and competencies. A customer at this level works hard, parties hard, works long hours, socializes on the weekends etc. We have combined two logical levels into one. The question that one asks at this level is 'What do they do? What are the skills that are required to use the product?'

Beliefs: This refers to the way the customer thinks. The customer could carry the belief that 'having a drink once in a while is a way to de-stress and socialize.' Perhaps he also believes that people who drink like to take risks, experiment, are independent thinkers, or are 'cool' and confident.

Identity: This is about 'who is your customer?' or 'what

is the identity of the customer?' The customer identifies himself as a rebel, a creative person, a decision-maker, a CEO or a bachelor. The demographic description is one way to identify the customer (for example, salary, sex, age, location). Psychographic profiling is another way to identify the customer.

Spiritual: This is about 'who else are like the customer?' They could straddle different professions such as artists, advertising professionals, software professionals, etc. They could cut across demographic identities such as single women, bachelors, married couples with no children, retirees, etc. They could include customers facing similar problems in different industry verticals. Insights could lead to the discovery of new market segments.

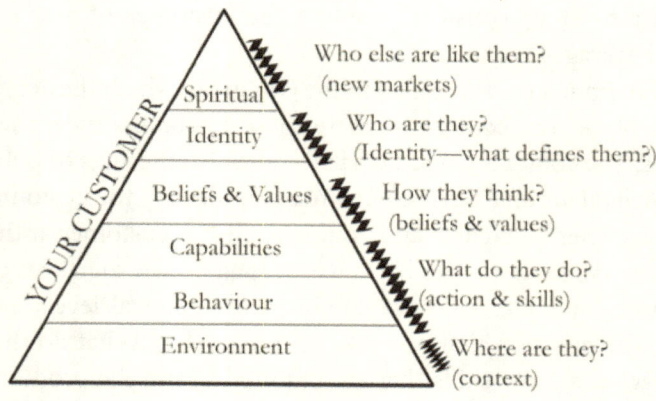

Fig 4.10: Understanding Your Customer

Exercise: You can use the above model to profile a customer who does the following:

- Purchases a BMW car.

- Subscribes to an online accounting solution for his small business.
- Purchases branded jewellery.
- Orders groceries online.
- Buys books regularly from Amazon.
- Buys a second-hand car even though he has money to buy a new car.
- Drinks coffee at Starbucks.
- Buys food at McDonalds.
- Buys cigarettes.

Needs-Context Relationship

The different market segments are determined by the various unique action-needs-interpretations-consequences (ANIC) combinations, subject to having an attractive market potential. The relationship between action, needs and context are illustrated in Fig 4.11.

If the usage context attracts sufficient number of customers, target the 'usage contexts' instead of the customers.

Businesses provide products or services so that customers can meet their needs. Customers use various strategies to take suitable action to meet the needs. The action takes place in a specific context. The action can be met by using different strategies. If the context can attract many customers, it will provide the business an opportunity to target customers by targeting their contexts. From the point of the view of a business, the context in which an action takes place provides an opportunity to offer a suitable strategy to the customer.

For example, Smirnoff, Kingfisher Premium, Black Dog, Heineken, Budweiser, etc., are different alcoholic beverages (strategies) that people consume (action) that meets their need for fun and entertainment, which means having such a cold beverage with friends that has positive consequences like deepening social bonds with friends and relaxation.

The question to be asked is 'are there contexts in which customers will come together to take similar action?' Can a context draw (or pull) potential customers to one place where they will take action that will translate into a purchase?

Let us continue exploring the example of the spirits and beverages company. It was noticed that most customers congregate and consume alcohol at corporate parties, clubs or private functions (weddings, birthday and social gatherings). The company has the option to assign a dedicated marketing person to look at contexts such as corporate events, private parties and social clubs. Instead of selling the product directly to the end consumer, the company can target the contexts where their product has a high likelihood of being consumed.

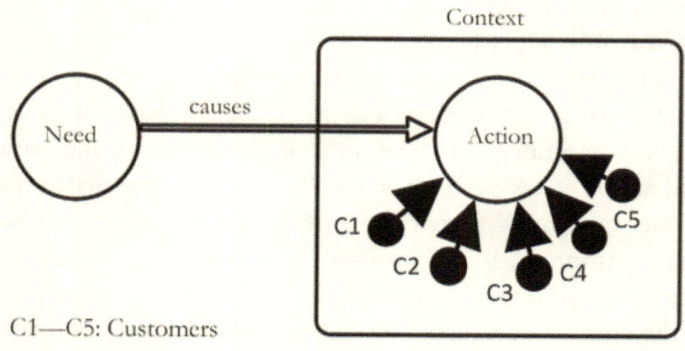

Fig 4.11: Needs-Context Diagram

Contexts attract customers. On the other hand, one could also identify routes to markets by pushing the offering through retail distribution channels. The spirits and beverages company is likely to have a mixed strategy of reaching the customer by targeting contexts and through retail outlets. They are likely to stock their products in retail stores, bars, hotels and also target contexts such as corporate events.

Exercise: Would the strategies below attract enough customers in a specific context? If yes, you can identify those contexts where the customer's needs are going to be met.

- An entry-level car (for example, Tata Nano)
- Bicycles
- Helmets
- Sports items such as a cricket kit, football, etc.
- Parenting workshops
- Yoga for women
- Food catering business
- Adventure sports
- Horoscope services
- Insurance products for the elderly
- Mutual Fund SIP (Systematic Investment Plans) products

Using channels to reach customers: As mentioned, one can use the push strategy of using distribution channels (wholesale-retail stores) to reach customers. Let us consider the drill example we had used at the beginning of the chapter.

Find below the list of likely customers who could purchase a drill to make a hole:

- Electricians
- Plumbers
- Carpenters

- Hobbyists/Individuals for self-help purpose

Potential customers with considerable market size are carpenters, plumbers and electricians. Where are they likely to buy the drill? Are there situations where they will come together? Are there conferences being held for this segment of customers where they can learn new skills, learn about new technologies or upgrade their products through special offers? If there are no attractive contexts where this segment of customers congregate, targeting contexts might not be attractive. Instead, retail outlets such as hardware stores, electrical shops, and large diversified hypermarkets might be an alternate channel to reach customers.

When there are insufficient number of customers that meet in a given context, it is a good idea to *focus on traditional retail channels rather than on contexts.*

Listed below are a few examples of actions and the possible contexts that would attract customers:

TABLE 4.5
Actions that Attract Customers to a Specific Context

Strategies	Context
Loose Flowers	Outside temples (India-specific), Near residential communities
Restaurant	Highways, malls
Pest Control	Apartment complexes, office complexes
Popcorn	Cinema halls, malls
Cakes	Birthdays, celebration parties
Customized T-Shirts	Clubs, colleges, corporate events
School Management Software	Principal and teacher conferences

Positioning Using Needs

Brand associations attempt to build strong connections between the offering and the need. For example, the Liril brand of soap is associated with freshness. Freshness is the meaning that was attached to the need for energy, health and cleanliness. Hindustan Lever, the company that owns Liril, targeted its marketing communication to associate the brand Liril with the idea of freshness. The advertisement carried a model bathing under a clear, free-flowing waterfall and evoked emotions attached to freshness. The visuals and the sounds reinforced the idea of freshness.

Exercise: Below are some well-known brands. What do you think their positioning statement is and what is the need that is met through the brand associations? What are the emotions that they evoke through their advertisements and print copy statements?

- Nike
- Facebook
- McDonald's
- Infosys
- Wipro
- Redbus
- Naukri
- Flipkart

Summary

In this chapter, we laid down a process of discovering the various components of met and unmet needs. We learnt to formulate the **complete needs statement** and the **complete unmet needs statement**, which captures the relationships between action-need-meaning and their consequences.

Dilts's logical levels are extensively used throughout this chapter, and its utility in understanding some of the concepts was highlighted through examples.

A framework of thinking was laid down to analyse the *decision-making criteria* used by customers to decide on a chosen strategy to meet a need. A model of thinking was also introduced to develop a customer profile based on Dilts's logical levels. The needs-context relationship has been highlighted to provide insights into how customers can be located based on the context of their use of the product.

CUNS is used to discover unmet needs and explore new opportunities. CNS is used to deepen one's understanding of existing customers and markets. A few exercises have also been provided to practise the application of the tools discussed in this chapter.

The process of discovering a customer's unmet needs helps in fine-tuning one's understanding of how customers think, behave and make decisions. The logical levels help in chunking down the meaning of needs and the consequences of action.

5

Disconnect Between Needs and Action

I attended a parenting talk recently, and the facilitator asked the audience, 'What would you like your children to become when they grow up?' Listed below are some of the aspirations that parents had for their children:

- Compassionate, kind and caring.
- Independent thinker.
- Honest, trustworthy and respected.
- Friendly and dependable.
- An assertive leader who speaks his mind.
- Have a steady job and earn lots of money.
- Be happy.
- Good in academics, sports, arts and music.
- Be empathetic and sensitive to others around.

Every parent wants all of the above for their children. However, the reality is different. When a child asks his parent, 'Dad, how does the airplane fly?' the enthusiastic father might start off on a lecture about thrust, lift, drag, gravity and how helicopters are different. Often, the child does not get the opportunity to think for himself. We are in a hurry to share our thoughts and experiences. We want our children

> Often, what we do in life is exactly opposite to what we want for ourselves in the long term.

to be independent, and yet we do not provide them the autonomy to make their decisions, even in matters such as the dress they wear to a party, the way they spend their pocket money, what they order in a restaurant and how they spend their time. *In our daily lives, what we do is exactly opposite of what we want for our children.*

Fig 5.1: When Intentions Are Positive

A leader is no different. He starts off a new assignment thinking, 'I need to create a team with members who will support one another, foster an environment where team members can express their thoughts freely, be recognized as an impartial, righteous and respected leader, mentor team members and provide a conducive environment for personal growth.' Often what happens is just the opposite. The leader takes sides, makes sarcastic remarks, is intolerant of opposing views, is self-centred and creates an environment of insecurity.

Same goes for organizations. The mission statement of an organization typically reflects the desire to meet long-term needs. But you will often come across situations where the employee's actions are not aligned with that mission. There are companies that insist on employees memorizing the mission statement and spewing it out when asked. If they can reproduce the statement, all is well. If not, it is assumed that they are not aligned with the organization's mission.

Fig 5.2 highlights the disconnection between long-term needs and current actions. The meaning attached to a need depends on the frame of reference. When a need is seen through a short-term time frame, its meaning and implications can be very different to viewing it through a long-term time frame. Conflict happens when short-term needs and actions are not in the interests of long-term needs.

> When action is caused by short-term needs, check if it meets your long-term interests.

The intentions are positive, but the actions are seldom in alignment with the long-term requirements of the person or the leader or the organization.

A few examples where the short-term needs and actions are not aligned with long-term needs are listed in Table 5.1.

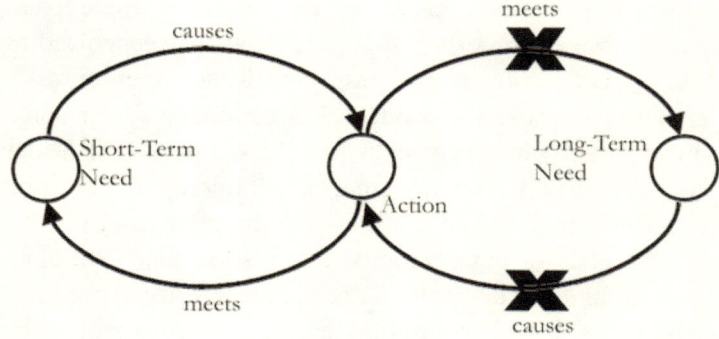

Fig 5.2: Disconnect Between Needs and Action

TABLE 5.1
Long-Term and Short-Term Needs and Actions

Needs	Meaning of Long-Term Need	Meaning of Short-Term Need	Action
LT: Health ST: Fun, Relationships	Eat less salty and oily foods. Eat foods that are lower in cholesterol.	To have fun watching a movie with family. To ensure that the host at the marriage party is not offended.	Have snacks during the interval break. Have buffet lunch at a wedding.
LT: Financial stability ST: Immediate gratification, To be seen	Save in long-term bank FDs, PPF. Invest in assets that will appreciate in value.	Maximize annual returns. Enjoy the moment and have fun right now.	Invest in stock markets. Buy high-end cars, lead flashy lifestyle, socialize in four-star hotels.

| LT: Honesty ST: Growth, Family well-being | Develop integrity, do not give and take bribes. Adhere to rules, transparency in dealings. | Passport required in the next four days. To ensure that my boss does not transfer me. | Bribe the government official to get things done quickly. Ingratiate oneself by overlooking lapses by boss in purchase deals. |
| LT: To be fair ST: Relationships, Protection, Security | Want to treat others fairly and be treated fairly by others. To promote meritocracy in all walks of life. | Ensure that the home is clean when the guests arrive. To please a powerful friend for a mutual favour. | To not give the housemaid leave when she is not keeping well. To offer the recommended candidate a job even though he does not fit the requirements. |

*LT: Long-Term, ST: Short-Term

This disconnection happens because of two main reasons:

- Short-term focus on immediate gains that are not aligned with long-term interests.
- Inability to link 'long-term needs' to the consequences of a specific action (lack of awareness of linkages).

Short-Term Focus: Disconnection happens when long-term needs are sacrificed for short-term gains. For example, a parent who wishes his child to be truthful and honest procures a false medical certificate so that his child can take three days off from school; a leader who wants to build an empowered organization does not delegate decision-making powers because of his insecurities; and an organization that wants to promote innovation does not allocate time and resources for R&D or take steps to foster innovation. These are instances when the *action-*

doers sacrificed long-term needs for short-term gains. The gains from current actions are just too attractive to override. You will come across cases of celebrities with poor money management skills, who end up splurging their hard-earned money and going bankrupt soon after. Their actions are geared towards fulfilling current needs that conflict with their long-term requirements.

Most of the problems that adults, leaders and organizations face can be traced to actions that were taken for short-term gains. Despite positive intentions, parents often act in total contravention to the long-term interests of the child resulting in permanent damage that manifests later as deviant behaviour. Organizations that make decisions that are misaligned to their long-term needs end up winding up their operations (for example Sony's Walkman, Kodak's camera, Polaroid, Blackberry). They ignored the need for innovation. Similarly, by the time a leader wakes up to his mistakes, his team members have already taken flight. It takes time to build a culture of trust, autonomy, empathy and empowerment in an organization, and it is important to ascertain the impact of any action on long-term interests.

The Story of Kodak Camera[6]

1884: American inventor George Eastman, who later becomes the founder of the Eastman Kodak Company, patents photographic film stored on a roll.

2009: After seventy-four years of production, Kodak stops selling the 35mm colour film.

2011: Kodak's shares fall by more than 80 per cent.

2012: Kodak files for Chapter 11 bankruptcy.

---

[6]*The Independent*, UK, dated 20 January 2012.

In February 2012, Kodak announced that it would cease making digital cameras, pocket video cameras and digital picture frames, and focus on the corporate digital imaging market. How did this happen?

In the 1990s, Kodak poured billions into developing technology for taking pictures using mobile phones and other digital devices. But it held back from developing digital cameras for the mass market for fear of killing its all-important film business. Others, such as the Japanese firm Canon, rushed in.

So, who invented the digital camera? Ironically, Kodak did it in 1975, long before the digital age or, rather, a company engineer called Steve Sasson, who put together a toaster-sized contraption that could save images using electronic circuits. The images were transferred to a cassette tape and were viewable by attaching the camera to a TV screen, a process that took twenty-three seconds.

It was an astonishing achievement. But Mr Sasson and his colleagues were met with blank faces when they unveiled their device to Kodak's bosses. Even they didn't see its full potential.

For Kodak's leaders, going digital meant killing film, smashing the company's golden egg, to make way for the new. Historians may one day conclude that most of the company's slow unraveling can be traced to the failure of its leaders to recognize the huge potential of Mr Sasson's invention.

Don Strickland, a former vice-president, left the company in 1993 because he couldn't persuade it to manufacture and market a digital camera. He put it this way: 'We developed the world's first consumer digital camera, but we could not get approval to launch or sell it because of fear of the effects on the film market.'

In other words, short-term gains took precedence over their long-term needs. They were fully aware of the choices but did not anticipate the impact of these decisions in the long term.

Lack of Awareness of Linkages: Sometimes, the leader or the parent is unaware of the implications of current actions on his or her long-term needs. You will find parents who are unaware of the impact of using derogatory language on the growth of a child, or a leader who is unable to see the link between his taking sides and his need for a safe, impartial working environment or an organization that is not able to see the link between the lack of investment in innovation and the organization's survival. It is this lack of awareness of the scope and extent of the impact of current actions that drives people, leaders and organizations to do things that are detrimental to their long-term interests.

Infosys, a large IT diversified software company, located in India, prides itself as a premium IT services provider with one of the highest net margins in the industry. It has long been a company policy that they will not do business at lower margins because it would dilute their brand image. However, post the 2008 global meltdown, many customers were facing serious cash flow problems, and IT budgets were under huge strain. Customers wanted to renegotiate existing contracts, and new customers wanted better deals. This would have meant doing business in the range of 17–20 per cent net margins. Refer to Table 5.2 for trends on net margins at four major India-based IT companies. Another company, CTS has not been included as it is listed in the US. As you can observe, all the competitors dropped their net margins substantially during the 2008–09 period to accommodate the requests of clients, except Infosys.

TABLE 5.2

Net Margins of Four Major Indian IT Companies

	2007	*2008*	*2009*	*2010*	*2011*	*2012*	*2013*	*2014*
Infosys	27.51	27.66	27.47	27.33	24.81	24.54	23.32	21.23
HCL	21.81	13.93	12.90	10.37	10.47	11.63	15.79	20.25
TCS	22.77	22.37	18.90	23.31	24.30	21.30	22.09	23.43
Wipro	19.53	16.33	15.13	16.89	19.52	17.48	17.73	17.95

Source: Trends of net margins from www.gurufocus.com

Given the 2008 crisis, Infosys had the following choices:

1. Adhere to the company philosophy of not doing low margin business that will dilute brand image.
2. Continue to move up the value chain and start looking at even higher margin businesses.
3. Pursue new large ticket deals and new customers by reducing the margins. The new contracts had the potential of impacting existing contracts.

Infosys opted for options one and two. They began to scale up their IT consulting division and competed with IBM and Accenture for big-ticket consulting deals. The margins in consulting were higher compared to traditional outsourced IT services.

Competitors sniffed an opportunity in reducing margins and started to pitch for big ticket services contracts ($50–100 million and more). They were willing to do business at 13–17 per cent net margins and provide an empathetic relationship with customers going through hard times. Potential customers began to respond positively to the support extended by these companies, and Infosys' competitors started to win big ticket deals. Some existing customers of Infosys moved over to these new service providers. By the time Infosys realized its mistake (their net margin had dropped to 24.8 per cent in 2011) they had already lost many deals. Infosys, which was once the bellwether of the IT industry, started to lose its sheen and failed to gain large contracts. In 3–4 years' time, Cognizant Technology Solutions, one of the competitors listed in the US, grew very rapidly and began to overtake Infosys and other large IT diversified companies by dropping their margins. For 5–6 years, Infosys stagnated with no clear direction. This inflexibility impacted the brand image, workforce turnover increased, employees were unhappy, morale was at its lowest and many senior people quit the organization. With new management in place, things are expected to improve at Infosys. In fact, the net margin for the year ending March 2016 was 21.6 per cent.

Infosys was not aware of the scope of impact of their current actions on their long-term need for a robust and empathetic relationship with its customers. They were focused on maintaining net margins and oblivious of their need for deepening relationships with customers. Empathy was missing from the way Infosys looked at the situation. By showing inflexibility in accommodating genuine client requests, it lost the opportunity to strengthen goodwill with its customers.

Macaulay Culkin: Parents Causing Long-Term Damage[7]

Born 26 August 1980 in New York, the super cute Macaulay was the third of eventually seven children. He began acting at the age of four and played the best parts in pretty much every amazing children's movie made at the time. By the age

---

[7]Source: Various sources from the Internet.

of nine, he was the cute, endearing star of *Home Alone* and *Home Alone 2*. He'd made enough money by twelve and quit acting at fourteen. He was living every child's dream!

A huge part of his decision was to spite his father, Kit, who, after buying a huge New York City townhouse (upgraded from a one-bedroom apartment), was still unhappy with Macaulay and his siblings, even though it was his young son's money that funded his new lavish lifestyle. Culkin said of his father, 'My father was overbearing. Very controlling. He was always the way he is, even before my success. He'd play mind games to make sure I knew my place.'

His parents finally divorced, both filing for custody, and both wanting control over Macaulay's $11 million fortune.

Knowing his father and mother, Patricia, wanted his money, the young child managed to stop his parents from getting their hands on his hard-earned cash, a move which led to his father no longer wanting to communicate with him.

Moving out of the limelight, Macaulay dropped out of school before finishing his senior year to marry his childhood sweetheart, Rachel Miner. They married when they were both just 17 in 1998 but separated in 2000, with their divorce being finalized in 2002. In 2004, he was arrested for possession of controlled substances including marijuana and Xanax. Macaulay began a dangerous descent into what looked like a debilitating drug addiction. However, he still appears in commercials, films and other gigs.

Here is a case of parents being overbearing and chasing short-term monetary gains at the cost of the long-term well-being of their child. The long-term damage that parents can sometimes cause, knowingly or unknowingly, can be disturbing. There are several cases of celebrities having had a tough childhood.

Conflict Based on the Lack of Understanding of Needs

Whenever Sonia walked into the office, she would see her

subordinate, Rahul, playing solitaire on his desktop or browsing sports websites to check out the latest cricket match score. Sonia was a workaholic and did not like the sight of Rahul using office time and resources to spend time on unofficial work. Rahul was a software engineer who completed any assigned work on time and considered the time he spent on games as relaxation.

Self-awareness is a journey inwards that can help in understanding the world outside.

Sonia wanted to let Rahul know that his usage of office resources was unacceptable. The next time she saw Rahul playing solitaire, she remarked, 'Rahul, have you completed the assignment that I gave you this morning?'

'I have started on the assignment, and I will complete it before tomorrow's end of day deadline,' Rahul replied.

'And what are you doing right now?' asked Sonia.

'Taking a break.'

'Taking a break? I thought you were whiling away your time. When I am in the office, I ensure that I am totally focused on office work. I would like you to focus on the work assigned to you,' remarked Sonia.

'Sure...but I am...'

'No ifs and buts, Rahul. Let us have some discipline in the office. I hope you are aware that you are violating the company rules on usage of office resources, as laid down in section 2(b) of the employment contract. The next time I come across any violation, I will be forced to act by the rules laid down by the company. By the way, I want to see the assignment on my table by the end of day,' interrupted Sonia and walked away.

Subsequently, Sonia started to focus on what Rahul was doing at the office, so much so that it became intrusive.

Rahul began to mistrust and dislike Sonia. Although he was an excellent team player, he began to lose interest in the job. Sonia started to see many more chinks in Rahul and gradually started to put down Rahul in front of others while side-lining him in team meetings. A jovial, amiable, brilliant Rahul became a disgruntled employee who quit the organization after a couple of months. Let us summarize what happened.

TABLE 5.3

Interpretation of Actions (B→A→C→D)

Sonia's Interpretation: [A]	Rahul's Action: [B]
Rahul is playing computer games and browsing sports websites in the office.	I have had a long day. I have completed most of the work assigned to me. My mind requires a break. Let me play solitaire and watch the latest sports news.
One must do only office-related work in the office.	
People using office resources for personal use demonstrates a lack of integrity.	*Feelings:* relaxed, tired and comfortable.
I work so hard and for long hours. Rahul is not bothered about the growth of the firm. He is selfish and irresponsible.	
Feelings: jealous, irritated, anxious and embarrassed.	
Sonia's Action: [C]	**Rahul's Interpretation:[D]**
Rebuke Rahul.	She is unreasonable.
Advance timeline to submit assignment.	Sonia did not even bother to hear my side of the story.
Walk away abruptly.	She is rude.
Put Rahul down in front of others.	*Feelings:* helpless, frustrated,
Feelings: satisfied, irritated and restless.	disturbed, gloomy and confused.

Sonia's interpretations of Rahul's actions and vice versa are shown in Table 5.3. Also listed are the possible feelings that both of them went through during this transaction. Sonia responded to Rahul based on her interpretation of Rahul's actions. In all likelihood, she was not aware of her thoughts and beliefs. The next time Sonia sees Rahul doing something similar, her belief about Rahul being irresponsible will be reinforced, thus determining her future course of action. It becomes a self-fulfilling prophecy. In this case, a frustrated Rahul had to resign.

Sonia's body language (walking out abruptly), words and tone impact the way Rahul forms his thoughts about the situation. Non-verbal communication is as important as spoken words.

Is there a way that Sonia and Rahul could address such issues in the future that is respectful of each other's needs? The OFNR model provides a framework that can provide clarity and build empathetic communication.

OFNR Model

The OFNR framework was developed by Dr Marshall Rosenberg, the founder of NVC (Non-Violent Communication). This framework for communication recognizes the needs and feelings of self and others, thus enabling an environment that is empathetic and nurturing. This understanding ensures respect for what others need and feel, thus doing away with put-downs, criticisms, judgements and blame.

We can look at this transaction through the OFNR framework given below:

OFNR Model

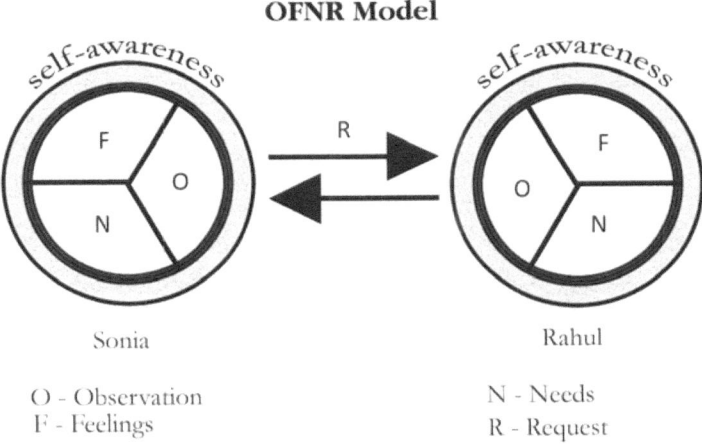

Sonia   Rahul

O - Observation   N - Needs
F - Feelings   R - Request

Fig 5.3: OFNR Model of NVC

'O' stands for observation without judgement. To separate the two is a difficult exercise (please note that this statement is judgemental!). It takes conscious effort to separate evaluation from observation. Jiddu Krishnamurti, the Indian philosopher, noted that observation without judgement is the highest form of human intelligence. We usually combine both of them in one sentence assuming that it is an observation. When we separate the observation from the evaluation, it helps us in generating new lines of action that are not dictated by our limiting beliefs.

The OFNR framework emphasizes becoming aware of our feelings and needs, as well as understanding what the other person is feeling and needing. With this understanding, the last step is to make a request for action or connection that is empathetic.

Let us apply this framework to the given situation:

Sonia's Self-Awareness	Awareness About Rahul
Observe oneself: muscles are tense, heart is beating faster, and breathing heavily.	*Observation of Rahul:* Rahul is playing computer games during office hours. He is not doing office-related work. *His Needs:* efficiency, effectiveness, rejuvenation and rest.
Her Needs: Integrity, responsibility and commitment. *Her Feelings:* jealous, irritated, anxious and embarrassed.	*His Feelings:* relaxed, calm and comfortable.

Once Sonia recognizes that Rahul's need for effectiveness and rejuvenation is met by taking regular breaks from office work, it will provide her insights into his actions. When Rahul is playing games, he is more relaxed and less stressed. Playing games is a stress buster for him. Sonia is also aware that Rahul is an efficient worker who meets his deadlines. With this understanding, Sonia is likely to respond differently:

Sonia: 'Hi, Rahul! It appears that you are enjoying the game.'

Rahul: 'Yes. I have two more levels to reach the master stage. I am almost there.'

Sonia: 'I guess playing games makes you more relaxed.'

Rahul: 'Very true. It energizes me, and it is fun.'

Sonia: 'I hope you have not forgotten the assignment I had given you.'

Rahul: 'Definitely not! I will be completing the assignment well ahead of the deadline.'

Sonia: 'Well, it is reassuring to know that you have not

forgotten the assignment deadline! Rahul, it is interesting how these games help in de-stressing and energizing people at work. However, I am concerned about office resources used for personal work. It violates the company rules on usage of office resources. This issue has been troubling me for some time. I am hoping for inputs from you on how we can find alternatives without violating office rules. Any thoughts you wish to share on this?'

Rahul: 'How about changing the rules to allow staff to use the resources for a limited period?'

Sonia: 'Yes, that is one perspective. Are there other solutions that will ensure that the needs of the organization are met?'

Rahul: 'I guess monitoring the usage of office resources could be a challenge. Well, I can't think of any alternatives right now.'

Sonia: 'What are the other things that could help de-stress and energize you?'

Rahul: 'Hmm… At home, I have coffee while working on something. That stimulates me.'

Sonia: 'That is interesting. How would you like to have a coffee break instead of playing games or browsing the Internet?'

Rahul: 'That will be great! But we do not have any cafeteria facility in our office.'

Sonia: 'Let me talk to my boss and check if the company can install a coffee vending machine for employees. Let me do a hard sell to get the facility at a subsidized rate!'

Rahul: 'You can count on my support for the proposal!'

Sonia: 'Thanks. Meanwhile, I want you to gradually put a stop to using the office computer for personal use before this weekend. I am looking for your support and understanding in ending this activity so that we do not violate the spirit of the company rules.'

Rahul: 'I understand the need for following company rules. I was not aware of the scope of these rules, and I will work towards finding alternative solutions. I am hoping that we can get the coffee vending machine soon!'

When Sonia and Rahul understand each other's perspectives, needs and feelings, and make an appropriate request of one another, it leads to a win-win situation for everyone. The decision becomes consensual rather than imposed. Sonia and Rahul's accountability increases because both of them feel a sense of ownership about the decision.

What would happen if only one of them was applying the OFNR model to communicate? The situation would still be better off than a situation where both the parties are not empathetic. When one party is empathetic, the other person will cool down and respond in a way that improves the situation.

Moralistic Judgements

Suresh and Ravi belonged to the sales department of a start-up that provided subscription-based online accounting solutions through a SaaS model to micro enterprises in India. There were multiple subscription plans starting from ₹400 per month to ₹1,200 per month, with customers having the option to pay quarterly or half-yearly or yearly in advance. The company's challenge was to reach micro enterprises (largely an unorganized segment) and keep the cost of sales to a minimum. Suresh thought that the best way to do this would be to hire a few sales executives who could follow up on leads by physically meeting the customers. Since accounting for an enterprise

'There is nothing either good or bad but thinking makes it so.'
—William Shakespeare

is a high involvement product, he thought they should meet customers personally to do a demo and close the deal. He wanted to develop channel partners who would be responsible for implementation of the solutions. However, Ravi was of the opinion that their low prices did not warrant investment into sales personnel and that the best way to target, engage and close customers was by using online marketing such as social media and Google Ads. A focus on online marketing required online demos, training and support—all of which could be centrally managed. Software to support an online ticketing system, webinars for demos and hiring online sales and support staff were core to this idea. Their conversation went along the following lines:

'That *will not work*. The cost of customer discovery and sales is very high,' remarked Ravi on hearing about Suresh's idea.

'Accounting is a high involvement product and customers expect sales personnel to do a demo and understand their requirements before purchasing the product. Offline sales calls are the *only way* that this is going to work. Online sales will not work for this kind of solution,' replied Suresh.

'I have seen similar solutions working well with online sales. You have not worked in this domain and will not know about its effectiveness,' retorted Ravi.

'Can you give me some examples where this worked?' Asked a visibly irritated Suresh.

Ravi could not immediately provide suitable examples.

'See. I told you so. The examples are not appropriate. The problem is that you make statements without any substantiation,' remarked Suresh.

This resulted in a heated argument that did not help in deciding a course of action. It became ugly, with the likelihood of creating permanent mistrust between the two. It was no longer a disagreement. It had become a conflict with the potential of damaging relationships and performance at the workplace. Conflict results in distrust, hostility and suspicion. Conflict happens when there are unmet needs or when others are seen to be obstructing the goals of a person. It involves a struggle for power and control.

Conversations like the above can impair or even scuttle the decision-making process and subsequent actions. Communications that use judgements that imply rightness or wrongness on the part of people who do not agree with our values create negative energy that does not help to manage conflicts. But communication is also a powerful tool that can help in resolving a difference of opinions. Use of phrases such as 'will not work', 'the only way', 'not appropriate', implies a lack of choice, blame and wrongness. This is a trap that leads to confrontation. Moralistic judgements such as blame, put-downs, labels, or criticisms tend to classify actions and people with labels like good, bad, smart, dumb, irresponsible, obstinate, or sensitive. This does not help in resolving conflicts.

Summary

Whether it is a parent or a leader or an organization, it is important to note the following:

- Write down your long-term needs (or mission) and internalize it. Chunk it down to specifics.
- Pause and reflect on any action in a given situation that you think can adversely impact your long-term needs.
- Once the awareness sets in, write down the short-term and long-term consequences of the action. Exercise the appropriate choice of action with full awareness.

- Develop a mechanism for reflection, learning from the past and making course corrections by taking pro-active steps to align actions to long-term interests.
- Learn new skills of empathetic communication such as the OFNR model of NVC.

Avoid moralistic judgements that are likely to be perceived as criticisms.

While evaluating choices of action, it is important to check alignment of the action to your long-term and short-term needs. Some benefits may seem very attractive in the short term but may be detrimental in the long term. Building empathetic organizations requires people to be treated as people and not as objects. Communication that reflects empathy is a skill that can contribute to the overall 'happiness index' of individuals and organizations.

6

Entrepreneurial Dilemma:
Pioneer or Follower?

Thomas has a peculiar habit. His decision to watch a movie in a cinema hall depended on the feedback he received from friends who had already seen the movie. When he had to admit his child to a play school, he made several enquiries with parents whose kids went to that specific school and checked out online reviews before making the decision. This pattern of decision-making extended to many aspects of his life. In the workplace, he would first wait for someone else to take the initiative in doing something, wait until he had sufficient information on that person's experience, analyse the data and decide for himself the most suitable line of action.

There are people who need to know everything there is to know about an assignment before taking it up. In the case of any uncertainty, they will wait for more data rather than be the first one to experience the problem. You could call them conservative or wise. On the other hand, there are entrepreneurs who jump at an opportunity without really digging deep into likely problems. They go with the attitude, 'I will handle it when I get there.' You could call them explorers or foolhardy. There is no right or wrong way to do things, but the above two approaches can be useful in different circumstances.

'Away From' versus 'Towards To' Strategies

There are two decision-making approaches that people use, these are illustrated below:

Focused on the centre
to avoid less than maximum
points: Away From.

Sometimes you are motivated
towards a target because it is
appealing and enjoyable.

Sometimes you are motivated
towards a target to avoid
something.

Focused on the centre
to get maximum points:
Towards To.

Fig 6.1: Dart Board Diagram Illustrating Thinking Patterns

As shown in Fig 6.1, the dart thrower aims for the centre of the dartboard, but the way he thinks about the target can vary. You can get insights into the way he thinks by observing the way he is feeling. One way to think about the target is—'I will aim for the centre of the board as I can earn maximum points.' This pattern is called the 'towards to' thinking pattern. Another way of thinking is—'I will aim for the centre of the board to avoid getting less than maximum points.' This pattern is called the 'away from' thinking pattern. The 'towards to' thinking pattern focuses on *what can I get* by aiming for the centre, whereas the 'away from' thinking pattern focuses on *what needs to be avoided*. When the mind is focused on things that must be avoided, this becomes a distraction. This distraction is a discomfort that the person wants to move away from, and this causes *stress*.

Here are a few more examples. A child says, 'I am aiming for above 80 per cent,' while another child remarks, 'I am aiming to get not less than 80 per cent.' A person who wants to get married is looking for a life partner who is 'lively and full of energy', while somebody else is looking for a person who is 'not boring'. There are different ways of looking at the same situation, but in many areas of life, we are not even aware of the patterns we employ to make decisions.

Observe yourself and identify your predominant decision-making pattern. It will help you express your needs with more clarity.

In most people, one of these two decision-making patterns is prominent. For instance, a software bug fixer focuses on what is wrong with the software program. He focuses on the problems in the code rather than what is right about the code. A criminal lawyer is trained to focus on the loopholes in the arguments of the plaintiff. Similarly, an auditor focuses on the errors in recording financial transactions. A stockbroker needs to know when to sell shares and limit his losses (cut loss strategy). To be an effective stock broker, it is not good enough to know when to book profits. It is equally important to know when to limit one's losses. One can be successful by focusing on 'away from' strategies.

In a presentation, participants who make statements such as 'This would not work because…' or 'I see a problem here' exhibit an 'away from' pattern of decision-making. If you prefer the 'towards to' pattern, you are likely to find this irritating. If you are the presenter, this could seem like a roadblock to your plan. You would prefer to go ahead with the plan and solve problems as and when they occur. In such cases, when it appears that there is a difference in approaches to an issue, awareness about the different patterns that people use to make decisions would be helpful in non-personalizing the issue. In a given situation, both these perspectives can be important. The 'away from' approach wants you to be cautious and analyse all the expected problems. As the future cannot be predicted, the 'towards to' approach would like you to move forward and not get caught up with too much analysis. The emphasis is on moving forward towards the goal and handling issues as and when they are expected to occur.

You can discover your decision-making pattern by say observing your reasons for going on a holiday. If you take a vacation because you need a break from the stress at office or want to make your family happy and ensure they don't get upset with you, you are

> Often, people articulate what they don't want, seldom do they clearly articulate what they want.

exhibiting an 'away from' decision-making pattern. If you take a vacation because you love to travel, meet people and learn about different cultures and customs, you are exhibiting 'towards to' decision-making pattern.

Even in entrepreneurship, there are those who take the plunge (first movers), and there are others who wait and watch before stepping in (followers).

Fig 6.2: Pioneers Like to Do What Others Have Not Done Before

Who has the advantage here, the first mover or the follower? The first mover's advantage lies in the fact that he can be known as the *pioneer,* can capture mind share and market share in a new market. However, he has to spend more time and resources in understanding the real needs of the customer, pivot the business (if required), experiment with product offerings and discover customer value. He is a pioneer in the true sense and opens up the doors for others. If the customer's cost of switching over to a competitor's products is high, the first mover has a sustainable competitive advantage. Followers have the advantage of learning from the experiences of the pioneer, spending less time and resources and having more information to help fine-tune their products and solutions for specific markets. Resources that were spent on experimentation and pivoting can be spent on building mind and market share.

There are many instances where the first movers became the industry leader: Coca-Cola, eBay, Amazon and Kleenex are all such examples. On the other hand, there are several examples of pioneers being replaced by better versions of the product. For example, VisiCalc, the first spreadsheet program, was replaced by Lotus 1-2-3, and subsequently, Lotus 1-2-3 was replaced by Microsoft Excel. In fact, Microsoft is a good example of a company that has not been the pioneer in developing some of its popular products. The original DOS was purchased by Bill Gates from Seattle Computer Products for $50,000 and licenced to IBM. Netscape was a pioneer in web browsing that lost out to Microsoft's Internet Explorer. Dumont was the leader in selling TV sets but lost out to latecomers like RCA and Motorola. Chux was the leading disposable diaper but lost out to Procter & Gamble's Pampers. Ampex was the leader in video recorders for two decades until Sony took over.

Sony's Walkman was the leader for mobile audio players until the entry of iPod. There are many instances where the first mover advantage was eroded over time.

In an article in HBR (April 2005) by Fernando Suarez and Gianvito Lanzolla, the authors identified two factors that influence a first mover's fate: the pace at which the technology of the product in question is evolving, and the pace at which the market for that product is expanding. Knowing how fast or slow the technology and the markets are moving will allow you to understand your odds of succeeding with the resources you possess.

Now that you have examples on either side of the fence, it becomes even harder to decide if you want to become the pioneer or the follower.

If You Are a Start-up, What Should You Be Doing?

Consider the following situation: After extensive research and immersion studies of the marketplace, you have identified a gap in the market that presents an exciting business opportunity. You are thrilled about the idea but are not sure if the market size is attractive enough because it is an unorganized segment. You are aware of the large investments required in identifying and reaching out to the customer. Should you take the plunge or wait for someone else to take the first step so that you can enter at a later time?

For example, after consulting your mentors and advisors, the recommended course of action is to take the plunge immediately. However, your decision-making patterns are that of a follower. You are uncomfortable with the idea of taking the first step. There is a conflict between the pattern you usually follow and the decision that needs to be made in the current circumstances. What will you do? Follow your old pattern and be comfortable or switch over to an uncomfortable one?

Challenging the Pattern

When you come across such a situation, ask yourself what needs are being met by either of these decision-making patterns and check your willingness to move out of the comfort zone of your preferred pattern. Do this before beginning to evaluate the choices. Your mind needs to be at peace with your decision. This clarity will ensure that you give your 100 per cent towards the choice that you make rather than search for excuses if your choice doesn't end up working out.

The needs that a pioneer meets by getting into entrepreneurship are innovation, creativity and adventure. The meaning of these needs is likely to do things that no one has done before or create solutions that can change the world. The follower has additional needs, for *predictability* and *structure*. The priorities of these needs are different for the follower and the pioneer.

After identifying the needs, it is important to question the beliefs about these needs. For example, what specifically do you mean by predictability or structure? If there is evidence to prove that predictability with certainty is an elusive concept, the entrepreneur is likely to move out of the comfort zone and accept unpredictability as a natural corollary of any entrepreneurial venture.

Growth and Congruence

In our personal lives and in business, there is a desire to grow. Growth represents change. And change impacts the surroundings. Any change that is oblivious to the requirements of the surrounding environment will result in imbalanced and incompatible growth.

If businesses grow at the cost of the environment, it results in short-term benefits for the enterprise at the cost of long-term adverse impact on the environment. This damage will begin to impact the business and its constituents in quick time. Growth has to be inclusive. It needs to incorporate the needs of various constituents, not just owners and customers.

> 'If you look at what you have in life, you'll always have more. If you look at what you don't have in life, you'll never have enough.'
> —Oprah Winfrey

When we refer to business growth, we are interested in the following:

- What is the interpretation of growth for the business?
- How does one grow? What are the factors responsible for growth?
- What is the expected rate of growth?
- Impact of growth on the system (self, competition, industry structure, supply chain, customers, etc.)

Let us look at these aspects of growth:

Interpretation of Growth

For a business entity, growth could mean an increase in sales, higher margins, an increase in the number of customers acquired, an increase in market share or increase in GMV (Gross Merchandise Value). In the e-commerce industry, the barometer of growth is the GMV. Goods are sold online at deep discounts to increase the GMV with the intention of increasing the customer base even if the transactions are not profitable. It is commonplace for goods to be sold below cost price. For this to happen, hundreds of millions of dollars have been invested in the e-commerce sector, and this has resulted in frenetic growth rates.

There are companies that measure growth as a share of the market. Market share is a relative measure and depends on how competition fares in the marketplace. Growth needs to be defined in a way that can be understood by everyone in the organization. A measurable quantity lends itself to the diffusion of the idea across the organization and also helps in allocating resources appropriately. Growth could be a combination measure, for example, increase in sales and net profit margins.

Non-profit organizations, as their name suggests, do not equate growth to profitability. Their metrics of measurement could be the number of children covered by the free food distribution scheme, the number of houses built for poor people or the decrease in the number of cases of malarial diseases in a geographic location.

When a mother refers to the growth of her child, she usually refers to intelligence (as she interprets it), maturity, development of motor skills, language skills, social interactions, independence in actions or confidence. Most of the growth parameters are qualitative. A parent is unlikely to refer to growth as a measure of academic performance at school. Similarly, business growth is not just about an increase in sales, profits, margins, market share, but also needs to include initiatives in areas such as family welfare, emotional intelligence, social responsibility initiatives and work-life balance programs. This balanced approach enables businesses to build a strong foundation for healthy growth in all aspects of a business and society. CSR initiatives are meant to meet exactly this need for an organization's inclusive growth.

CSR Initiatives of Famous Companies[8]

Corporate Social Responsibility refers to the way businesses are managed to bring about an overall positive impact on the communities, cultures, societies and environments in which they operate.

In India, under the Companies Act, 2013, any company having a net worth of ₹500 crore or more, or a turnover of ₹1,000 crore or more, or a net profit of ₹5 crore or more has to spend at least 2 per cent of last three years average net profits on CSR activities. These rules came into effect on 1 April 2014.

Given below are a few examples of companies that have active CSR programs:

Mahindra & Mahindra

Mahindra Pride Schools provide livelihood training to youth from socially and economically disadvantaged communities and have trained over 13,000 youth. M&M sponsors the Lifeline Express trains that take medical treatment to far-flung communities. There's also the Project Hariyali, which has planted 7.9 million trees to date, including four million trees in the tribal belt of the Araku Valley. It has constructed 4,340 toilets in 1,171 locations across eleven states and 104 districts, specifically for girls in government schools, as part of 'Swachh Bharat Swachh Vidyalaya'. Expenditure on CSR in the last fiscal year was ₹83.24 crore—2 per cent of PAT.

Tata Steel

CSR activities are focused on education, healthcare, facilitation of empowerment and sustainable livelihood opportunities, preservation of ethnicity and culture of indigenous communities and sports. Initiatives run across ten districts in Jharkhand, Odisha and Chhattisgarh, covering nearly 500 villages. Total spending in 2014–15 on CSR was ₹171.46 crore, which is 2.04

---

[8]Source: *The Economic Times* and www.business2community.com

per cent of the average net profit of the last three fiscal years.

Starbucks

Starbucks has been around for more than four decades, and the company looks for better ways to develop sustainable production of its coffee. It has set in place some guidelines which it calls C.A.F.E Practices, ensuring environmental leadership, economic accountability and product quality. Starbucks also supports Ethos Water, which provides clean water to more than a billion people.

Nu Skin

Nu Skin (Personal Care Company) runs initiatives called 'Nourish the Children'. The program was started in 2002 and allows company sales leaders, employees and customers to donate nutrient-rich meals to needy children. In March 2014, Nu Skin announced that it had surpassed 350 million donated meals. The company also operates the Force for Good Foundation, which works to offer children relief from illiteracy, disease and poverty.

Microsoft

Microsoft has its annual Employee Giving Campaign, where employees attend fundraising events for non-profit organizations. The campaign has been held every year since 1983 and has raised more than $1 billion in contributions to more than 31,000 organizations.

How Does One Grow?

What motivates someone to seek growth? Is it a fundamental aspect of all living things? All living things grow without any conscious effort. It appears to be a natural progression of life. Growth is a *core need* that can motivate people and organizations into action. In the business context, what is important is not the size of the performance metrics but the *momentum* of growth. Companies (public and listed) are valued-based on expectations of growth. Higher valuations help companies raise more money at lower costs, and the investment community closely monitors growth rates. On the other hand, a private limited company may not be necessarily seeking growth once it reaches a sustainable critical size. Lack of pressure to raise funds, niche market operations, business structure, and lack of resources, could be some reasons why smaller firms are not motivated to seek growth aggressively.

After understanding what growth is, the next logical question is 'how to grow'. This question is about *strategy* and *execution* and requires an understanding of the underlying factors that contribute to growth. Let us take an example.

Growth Objective: Increase sales by 30 per cent this year

Sales = Price × Volume

Table 6.1
Identifying Causes for Growth

What causes growth?	Increase in sales (for this example).
What causes sales to increase?	Price increase or volume increase or both.
What causes prices to increase?	Higher demand, lower supply. Increase in perceived value. Competition. Increase in raw material cost. Regulatory issues—increase in excise, duties, sales tax. Increase in cost of sales, for example, channel costs.
What causes volume to increase?	Higher demand. Change in consumption patterns. Discovery of new markets.

Table 6.1 provides insights into the factors that contribute to growth. There are three options to increase sales:

- Increase price, keep volume constant or slightly lower the volume.
- Keep price constant or slightly lower the price, increase volume.
- Increase price and increase volume.

To increase volume, you could continue to look for new geographical markets, customer segments or consumption patterns. If you can introduce a product variant in smaller packs (for example, shampoos, noodles, pickles, sauce, etc.), it could open up a new market because there are consumers who consume the products in smaller amounts.

To increase the price of the product, you will have to provide enhanced value to the customer through product innovation. For example, if you are in the motor cars business, this could require you to consider product variants such as a family car, an SUV, a sports car, a BMW, etc., to meet the needs of different customer segments.

The choice of strategy lies in understanding the strengths, weaknesses, execution capabilities, and internal operational efficiency of your organization, as well as external factors such as the supply chain (distribution channels and logistics), consumer behaviour, market access and regulatory compliances.

Rate of Growth

The rate of growth needs to be measurable. It is stated as a percentage increase or decrease with reference to a specific date, for example, 10 per cent growth in sales over the last quarter, annualized growth rates, per cent decrease in the number of cases of malarial fever in the last year, etc.

Some entrepreneurs want to grow fast. Quick growth requires spending a huge amount of money for high impact growth that raises expectations. The rationale for doing this is that it's better to spend huge amounts right now, capture the market and raise barriers to entry for other entrants. This approach can swing either way. If growth does not happen at the expected rate, investors might rather close the business than continue to lose money. You will find many businesses where millions of dollars have been invested, and the venture closes after a couple of years.

> Rapid customer acquisition without adequate focus on profitability is likely to end up in severe cash flow problems. This can be acute if the cost of customer switching loyalties is very low.

Higher growth rates also mean having internal systems that need to keep up with the soaring pace of growth. All systems and processes need to be scalable. The impact on people is also substantial. The higher expectations from the whole system require employees to be able to absorb higher levels of stress. If existing systems are not geared towards rapid growth, it is going to be difficult to meet the expectations of internal and external customers. It also requires people to develop mindsets which are distinctly different from ones where growth is normal. Huge investments do not necessarily mean increased profitability.

On the other hand, there are others who prefer incremental growth. Incremental growth is a conservative bet since it requires a smaller amount of resources, more time for resources (internal and external) to align with this growth and flexibility to pivot if things need course correction. This growth preference is less stressful on the whole system.

The disadvantage is that competition with deeper pockets can capture the market more quickly and raise your cost of sales.

Since rapid growth puts stress on various systems within the company, it is recommended to have a mixed growth pattern wherein growth periods are tempered by a consolidation period as shown in Fig 6.3. The consolidation period provides time to reflect, take stock of internal systems, fine-tune resources and energize the whole system to gear up for the next phase of growth. The consolidation period can be shorter than the growth period. Higher growth rates are not sustainable over long periods of time and are bound to taper off.

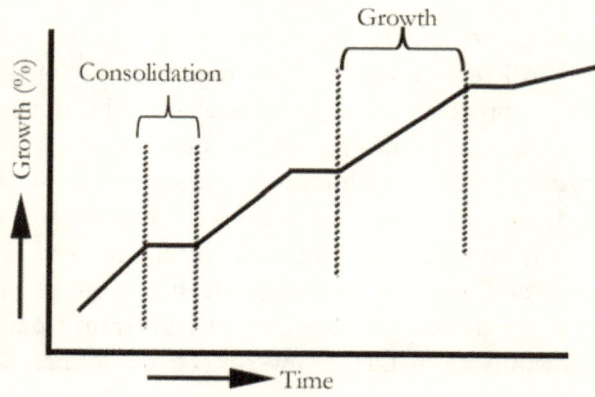

Fig 6.3: Mixed Growth Pattern

Inside Amazon: Wrestling Big Ideas in a Bruising Workplace[9]

This is a company where frenetic growth for many years places a lot of stress on its people.

At Amazon, workers are encouraged to tear apart one another's ideas in meetings, toil long and late (emails arrive past midnight, followed by text messages asking why they were not answered), and held to standards that the company boasts are 'unreasonably high'. The internal phone directory instructs colleagues on how to send secret feedback to one another's bosses. Employees say it is frequently used to sabotage others.

Many of the newcomers filing in on Mondays may not be there in a few years. The company's winners dream up innovations that they roll out to a quarter-billion customers and accrue small fortunes in soaring stock. Losers leave or are fired in annual cullings of the staff. Some workers who had suffered cancer, miscarriages, and other personal crises said they had been evaluated unfairly or edged out rather than given time to recover.

Bo Olson was one of them. He lasted less than two years in a book marketing role and said that his enduring image was watching people weep in the office, a sight other workers were familiar with as well. 'You walk out of a conference room and you'll see a grown man covering his face,' he said. 'Nearly every person I worked with, I saw cry at their desk at some point.'

In interviews, some said they thrived at Amazon precisely because it pushed them past what they thought were their limits. Many employees are motivated by 'thinking big and knowing that we haven't scratched the surface on what's out there to invent,' said Elisabeth Rommel, a retail executive who was one of those permitted to speak.

'A lot of people who work there feel this tension: it's the

---

[9]Jodi Kantor and David Streitfeld, *The New York Times*, 15 August 2015.

greatest place I hate to work,' said John Rossman, a former executive there who published the book, *The Amazon Way*.

Google and Facebook motivate employees with gyms, meals and benefits like cash handouts for new parents—'Designed to take care of the whole you,' as Google puts it. Amazon, though, offers no pretense that catering to employees is a priority. Compensation is considered competitive—successful mid-level managers can collect the equivalent of an extra salary from grants of a stock that has increased more than tenfold since 2008.

Amazon employees are held accountable for a staggering array of metrics, a process that unfolds in what can be anxiety-provoking sessions called business reviews, held weekly or monthly among various teams. A day or two before the meetings, employees receive printouts, sometimes up to 50–60 pages long, several workers said. At the reviews, employees are cold-called and pop-quizzed on any one of those thousands of numbers.

Impact of Growth on Ecology of Markets

Any growth activity impacts the environment and the ecology of the markets. High growth also requires people to work under tremendous stress, and this requires flexible and friendly HR policies that cover employees and their families. The whole supply chain comprising suppliers and vendors is required to gear up for the demands of growth.

Efforts to achieve higher growth rates require adequate responses from various partners in the supply chain. The industry structure is likely to undergo changes. Partners and competitors who cannot keep up with the pace of change are likely to fall behind and regress. Expansion of the market is also likely to attract new and large entrants. The challenge will always be to sustain the growth rate.

Inclusive Growth through Congruence

Individuals have needs that they are constantly trying to meet:

- Autonomy
- Competence
- Purpose
- Peace
- Connectedness
- Acceptance

The above six are some of the key drivers that motivate people. When organizations strive to meet the above needs, they achieve congruence between the needs of the individual and the needs of the organization. This leads to congruent growth.

If there is no congruence, any growth that happens will crumble from the inside over time. The business enterprise cannot control what happens in the market. However, it certainly can take ownership for matters inside the organization.

The above needs can be met through various strategies, such as delegation of powers across the organization, training and skill enhancement activities, internalizing organizational values, ensuring a healthy environment where people can share ideas, questioning without fear of reprimand or rebuke, building bonds among employees that enable people to connect to one another, accepting people unconditionally, and respecting people based on who they are and not what they necessarily do in the office.

There are organizations where ideas can come from any employee, and if the idea is found to be exciting, the employee is given enhanced responsibility to manage and own the idea. In Amazon, even relatively junior employee can make major contributions. The new delivery-by-drone project announced in 2013 was co-invented by a junior-level engineer named Daniel Buchmueller. Stephenie Landry, an operations executive in Amazon, joined discussions about how to shorten delivery times and developed an idea for rushing goods to urban customers in an hour or less. One hundred and eleven days later, she was in Brooklyn directing the start of the new service, Prime Now.

When you join Google, you will come across a deceptively laid-back corporate culture where the dress code is casual, you can play games, have snacks, enjoy a great variety of food across numerous cafeterias, relax on massage chairs, play foosball, visit the gym and have a haircut in a salon. You quickly realize that individual needs for acceptance, creativity, fun, autonomy and respect are adequately met in such organizations. There is congruence between what the employee needs and what the organization offers. This congruence gets reflected in the culture of the organization. In fact, one of Google's ten principle philosophies is 'you can be serious without a suit'. The material trappings are just an add-on. If a company were to copy all the material benefits without the spirit of congruence reflected in the organization's culture, it would fail to attract and retain talent.

How to Build a Motivated Team?

For any growth, you need a motivated team working towards the organization's goals. How does one motivate the team?

Rob is a highly talented software geek who founded a start-up along with Shyam, his batchmate from college. Shyam is the quintessential salesman—passionate, confident, persistent and customer-oriented. Both are hands-on people who are very detailed in their approach. They have a young team of thirty people and it is two years since they started operations.

Of late, they have observed that the employees were losing interest in their work. Rob believes that the growth of the firm is hampered by the lack of motivation among employees, and despite their best efforts, people were either leaving the firm or just floating around without any significant contribution. They realized that the employees were not taking initiatives, but were comfortable simply following and executing orders from the founders. Sacking people was a difficult proposition as they had spent a lot of time and money in training them.

'If you want to build a ship, don't drum up people to collect wood and don't assign them tasks and work, but rather teach them to long for the endless immensity of the sea.'
—Antoine de Saint-Exupéry

They decided to meet Arun, an HR consultant, to explore solutions to their problem. Arun met up with the employees separately to understand their perspectives. Arun, Rob and Shyam met to assess, understand the problem and explore solutions.

On being queried about the core issue, Rob defined their problem as, 'How do we motivate our employees to be excited and geared towards meeting the needs of the organization?'

'What have you done so far to motivate your team members?' asked Arun.

'As founders, we have given numerous pep talks, invited motivational speakers to share their experiences and instituted a reward system to recognize contribution and performance,' replied Rob.

'Did that work?' queried Arun.

'People are energized while listening to the talks and it lasts for a few days. But the impact wears off quickly. Most of them go back to their old habits in quick time. In fact, because of their sloppiness both of us end up doing their work. They do not seem excited about their work. They do not take initiatives, and look at their employment here as just another job,' replied Rob.

'And yes, the reward system brought forth its set of problems. Some employees got rewarded whereas others did not, and this caused resentment, jealousy and unhealthy competition amongst them. Some team members were seen to be the favourites of the founders, and there continues to be uneasiness in the air,' added Shyam.

'What makes you think you need to motivate them?' questioned Arun.

'As the founders, aren't we responsible for motivating them?' replied an agitated Rob.

'Let me reframe the question. What motivated you to start your entrepreneurial journey?' asked Arun.

'When we looked at the existing software solutions in the market, we realized that we had the expertise to build a world-class scalable product that would meet the customers' present and future needs. We wanted to bring about a change in the way customers worked towards solving their problems,' replied Shyam.

> 'I have been impressed with the urgency of doing. Knowing is not enough; we must apply. Being willing is not enough; we must do.'
> —Leonardo da Vinci

'I am hearing you say that you looked at yourselves as *change agents,* people who can make the world a better place. It perhaps met your need for challenge, creativity and innovation,' added Arun.

'Absolutely. We continue to look at ourselves that way,' replied Rob with a twinkle in his eyes.

'Did you have a boss to motivate you?' asked Arun.

'Hmm... Not really. Are you saying it is not necessary to have a boss to motivate employees?' remarked Rob.

'In other words, we were self-motivated. We found motivation and purpose inside of ourselves,' added Shyam.

'Exactly. In your words, you are as motivated now as you were earlier. This internal drive is called *intrinsic motivation.* Let me shed some more light on this,' Arun added and proceeded to explain the concept on the white board.

'Let me start with brass tacks. To be motivated means *to be moved* to do something. Not only do people have different amounts (levels) of motivation but also different reasons (orientations) to be motivated. The orientation of motivation focuses on the 'why' of actions. For example, a student can be highly motivated to do homework out of curiosity and interest or to impress a teacher or parent. The levels of motivation in both cases may be the same, but the reasons can differ.'

Fig 6.4 illustrates the ineffectiveness of external rewards after some time. 'Intrinsic motivation refers to doing something because it is inherently interesting or enjoyable and extrinsic motivation refers to doing something because it leads to a separable outcome (such as external rewards). Intrinsic motivation results in high-quality learning and creativity,' explained Arun. 'Let me give you an example. When George Mallory, the great mountaineer was asked, 'Why did you want to climb Mt Everest?' He replied, 'Because it is there!' For George Mallory, the motivation to do something was not driven by fame or by rewards. It was driven by the desire to challenge the human body and mind.'

'Let us do an exercise. For a moment, close your eyes and go

> 'All rewards, by virtue of being rewards, are not attempts to influence or persuade or solve problems together, but simply to control.'
> —Alfie Kohn

back to your childhood. Remember a time when you were excited about doing something, maybe doing a craft, solving puzzles, reading the encyclopedia, learning to ride a bicycle or playing your favourite game. What was it about the activity that excited you? Did you do it because of a reward attached to the activity? It has been observed that most of the things that we love doing are enjoyable and fun because we find them inherently interesting,' continued Arun.

'I forgot to add that the reward system we had put in place is no longer perceived to be motivating enough. We were mulling over making it even more attractive before we realized that we had better take expert advice on this issue. Regarding intrinsic motivation, I can relate to this,' remarked Rob, 'but clearly, we cannot become them. Is there anything we can do to make them intrinsically motivated?'

Fig 6.4: External Rewards Not Working

Wright Brothers: The Untold Story of the Airplane[10]

There was a race to build the first airplane at the end of the nineteenth century. Samuel Pierpont Langley, an astronomer, physicist, founder of the Smithsonian Astrophysical Laboratory and inventor of the bolometer, was a pioneer in aviation and was vigorously pursuing the task of building a machine that could fly. He was well-connected, well-funded and had assembled some of the best and brightest minds of the day. His PR was great, and the media followed him everywhere.

More than anything else, Langley wanted to be first. He wanted to be rich and he wanted to be famous. That was his driving motivation. Although well-regarded in his field, he craved the kind of fame Thomas Edison or Alexander Graham Bell enjoyed, the kind that comes only with inventing something big. Langley saw the airplane as his ticket to fame and fortune. He had plenty of cash, had government funding, was very smart, and had the best talent and ideal market conditions. Few of us today have heard of Samuel Langley.

A few hundred miles away in Dayton, Ohio, Orville and Wilbur Wright were also building a flying machine. Unlike Langley, the Wright brothers seemed to have the recipe for failure. They had no funding for their venture, no government grants, no connections and did not even have a college education! They funded their dream with the proceeds from their bicycle shop. None of the team members had a college education; some of them had not even finished high school. The difference between the Wright brothers and Langley was that they had a dream—they knew *why* it was important to build the thing. They believed that the flying machine would change the world. The problem of balance and flight challenged them, and the task was intrinsically motivating for

---

[10]Excerpts from *Start With Why: How Great Leaders Inspire Everyone To Take Action* by Simon Sinek, Portfolio, 2009.

the whole team. Langley was looking for achievement and did not have the Wright's passion for flight.

Orville and Wilbur preached what they believed and inspired the community to join them in their cause. Since they were driven with a strong sense of purpose, their series of mounting failures did not deter the team from working towards their mission. Every time the Wright brothers went out to take a test flight, so the stories go, they would take five sets of parts with them because they knew that's how many times they were likely to fail before deciding to come home for the day. On 17 December 1903, on a field in Kitty Hawk, North Carolina, the Wright brothers successfully flew their plane for fifty-nine seconds at an altitude of 120 ft. at the speed of a jog. This was all it took to usher in a new technology that would change the world.

The above example illustrates the power of being driven by intrinsic motivation and having a strong sense of purpose.

'You met with our employees. Is there something you can share with us?' asked Shyam.

'Oh yes! I have found the persons who are responsible for this state of affairs,' replied Arun.

'Rest assured you can give us the names of the employees. We would ensure that we do not take any harsh action against them. We would give them an opportunity to change. We are waiting to hear from you,' said an excited Rob.

'Well, the good news is that it is not your employees. The bad news is that *you guys are the problem*,' replied Arun.

'You must be joking!' remarked an aghast Rob.

'That is ridiculous. We are perhaps the nicest bosses anyone could have,' added Shyam, 'in fact, we encourage and lend support to our employees by doubling up and doing lots of stuff that they are supposed to be doing to ensure that the work gets done. We also give them credit so that it will motivate them to do better.'

'That is exactly one of the issues. Do you think they relish taking credit for something they have not done?' asked Arun.

'Hmm... You are making us think now. We have been under the impression that we were helping them. This discussion reminds me of my childhood where my mother used to do my homework. I remember handing over my homework and school projects so that she could complete it. When I was in seventh grade, my mother turned around and said—"You are old enough to do your homework." And I recall telling her—"How do I do it? All these years, you never gave me an opportunity to do my homework." It was a huge effort for me to get out of that pattern,' remarked a thoughtful Rob.

'Absolutely. You are doing the same with your employees now. Your help is likely to be construed as interference and does not help in empowering them to take decisions or do their own thing. Because they know you will find some gaps and complete the tasks by yourselves,' added Arun. 'Let me introduce you to the FROG model.'

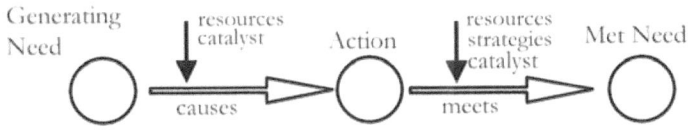

Fig 6.5: Catalyst—the FROG Requirements

'Refer to Fig 6.5. As an employer, you will have to supply the necessary strategies to your employees to help them meet their needs. The strategies could be specific tools, processes, conducive work environment, transparency in operations, or financial incentives. A catalyst in a chemical reaction is a desirable intervention that speeds up the reaction and energizes the whole system. The catalyst in the above figure refers to factors that energize people to work towards their goals. The FROG model consists of elements that act as catalysts. In their presence, the motivation to do something gets charged up significantly.

> If you are no longer having fun at work, you need to question and analyze the reasons. Remember, the only thing you can change, for sure, is yourself.

'To meet the need, a series of actions have to be taken. Each of the actions will help people get closer to meeting the goals. The catalysts will help the team move towards the goals with energy, enthusiasm and a sense of purpose. After talking to your team members, I discovered that the following are their most important unmet needs right now:

Unmet Needs of the Employees
Challenge: the tasks are not challenging enough.
Competence: inadequacy in skills required.
Autonomy: need to own tasks and take decisions.
Clarity: not clear about the long-term vision of the company.

'To understand the process of meeting these needs, the elements of the FROG model can provide some insights. The elements of the FROG model are below:

- Working towards the goals has to be **F**un and not a *chore*.
- Meeting the goal should be **R**ewarding.
- One needs to have a sense of **O**wnership of the goal.

- The actions have to be oriented towards meeting specific Goals.

'These elements constitute the FROG model and are *keys to motivation*. Every time you think of implementing a strategy, you can run your strategies through the FROG model, identify and execute actions that will motivate team members to work towards the goals,' explained Arun.

'I am already reflecting on some of our past actions and how we can do it differently. But is there anything specific that we are expected to do?' asked a confused Rob.

'The choice of strategies that you wish to provide would require a buy-in from the team members. Your interpretation is just one side of the coin. One way to get an employee buy-in is to involve the team members and make them define the broad parameters of the proposed strategy. That would provide them with a sense of ownership of the strategy and the outcomes,' explained Arun.

'I want more clarity on strategies. For instance, most jobs are bound to get monotonous sometimes. It is a challenge to make it interesting and keep people motivated. Can you suggest some strategies for making the job more interesting?' asked Rob.

'Sure. Since your team size is still small, you can experiment with some ideas such as cross-disciplinary learning, letting some back-end team members meet customers, getting customer testimonials on how your products make a difference to their operations or involve them in decision-making. These cross-disciplinary experiences can be effective in motivating people who are doing routine back-end operations such as support, maintenance and operations, without much of an idea of the impact of their work on customers,' replied Arun.

'Thanks for the insights. We will begin thinking on this right away and will keep you posted,' replied Rob.

More on the FROG Model

What is very important and is often not stated clearly is the importance of motivation orientation, the 'why we do what we do'. Even if you increase your motivation levels temporarily, if you do not have a valid motivation orientation, higher motivation levels will not be sustainable for long periods of time so long as the 'why' is ambiguous.

Ramesh was employed with a software company. He met project deadlines consistently, drew a decent salary, was a recognized star performer and got a bonus every year. He was in production support and was very good at his work. The spark was missing in his professional career. The job had become routine, and the fun element was missing. He was working with his head, but his heart was not in the job anymore. He forced himself to go to the office every day because he had a family to support. He was motivating himself to meet deadlines temporarily by using appropriate motivational strategies (by using an 'away from' strategy). But this was unlikely to last if he was not having fun in his job.

A five-year-old child no longer enjoys doing word puzzles because he is no longer having fun doing them. If your twelve-year-old is losing interest in doing maths that seemed interesting to him until he was eleven years old, it is likely that he is not having fun anymore. If that is the case, you need to dig deeper to understand the reasons for the missing fun element. At schools, children lose interest in subjects such as maths and science when the teacher makes the lessons dull, boring and intimidating. The responsibility to make learning fun is a huge challenge for teachers.

When there is a reward attached to doing something, we are 'moved into action'. Rewards can be tangible or intangible, internal or external, as long as the doer values them.

Sukhbir Singh was a first generation entrepreneur who came from a Punjabi family that was patriarchal. Key decisions at home were made by the head of the extended family (his father). The head of the family was looked upon with respect and at times with fear. His father was a man of few words who seldom praised people or expressed his emotions openly. Sukhbir was doing exceptionally well at his business and was making huge profits. But he was not happy; there was something missing. It soon transpired that he was looking for acknowledgement for his success from his father. His father had never bothered to acknowledge or praise Sukhbir's success,

Fig 6.6: When Things Are No Longer Fun

and that was hugely disappointing to him. And then one fine day, his father gave him a warm hug in front of a crowd at a function and said, 'I am proud that he is my son,' with tears in his eyes. For Sukhbir, this was perhaps the happiest moment of his life. It went beyond money or material wealth. The appreciation was a reward that made a great difference to him. *Intangible rewards* can be very effective.

Even a simple letter of appreciation on a piece of scrap paper from a boss to a subordinate can be a great motivator.

'O' is for ownership. One of the universal human needs is the need for *autonomy*. It refers to the sense of ownership and control over the desired outcome. Taking ownership means taking responsibility for one's actions. When there is a sense of ownership, this increases the intensity of moving towards achieving the goals. Ownership increases confidence in one's abilities.

> Often, intangible rewards can be very effective compared to tangible rewards. An understanding of the needs of team members will help you tailor appropriate rewards.

Some parents take decisions for their children on matters such as which TV program to watch, what kinds of books to read, what to eat in a restaurant, who to be friends with, when to study, what to study, or even whom to marry. If children are given the autonomy to take their own decisions starting from a very young age, it will help them become more confident and own up to their actions. It could be something as simple as letting them decide what dress they wish to wear, what time they play every day or what game to play. Research has shown that children having a sense of ownership of their outcomes have higher levels of intrinsic motivation.

Fig 6.7: Whose Goal Are You Meeting?

'G' stands for goal. As illustrated in Fig 6.7, it is important to check if the goals are your personal goals or the goals of someone else. In the business environment, employees need to set their goals so that they are accountable to themselves. Goals enable a person to focus his energy on tasks that are aligned with the goals. Having a goal can motivate a person to move confidently in a specific direction. Here is a famous quote from *Alice's Adventures in Wonderland*:

> 'Would you tell me, please, which way I ought to go from here?'
> 'That depends a good deal on where you want to get to,' said the Cat.
> 'I don't much care where—' said Alice.
> 'Then it doesn't matter which way you go,' said the Cat.

When you do not have a goal, whether written or unwritten, you are likely to be like flotsam, without any direction, drifting wherever the current takes you. When you have a goal, you are likely to focus your energies on achieving the goal and minimize dissipation of your energy into non-meaningful activities.

The next time you find your employee feeling low, you can ask yourself the following questions:

F: 'Is he having fun?'
R: 'What is the reward for doing the task? Is the reward of value to your employee?'
O: 'Does he have a sense of ownership of what he is doing?'
G: 'Does doing the task result in an outcome that he wants? Is it his goal?'

Summary

We follow different decision-making patterns. One of them is the mental pattern of a 'pioneer', and another is that of a 'follower'. We usually follow one of these patterns of decision-making in various situations. Identifying and being aware of your pattern will help you challenge the pattern when a major decision has to be made.

- Observe the way you have made decisions about various issues in the past.
- Note the pattern of decision-making that you usually follow.
- Identify the needs that are met by the decision-making pattern that you have followed.

We explored the idea of growth, inclusive growth through congruence and how to build a motivated team that will help you meet your need for growth. The FROG model was introduced to understand the elements that can energize someone to work towards a goal.

People tend to apply similar decision-making patterns in different contexts. Becoming aware of this pattern will help in working on oneself and also in developing a better understanding of patterns that others apply in their decision-making. The FROG model is a tool that encapsulates interesting aspects of various motivational theories and can be effectively applied to different circumstances.

7

Connectedness and Empathy

'Lonely' is an adjective that is used to describe the entrepreneurial journey. This is often used in the context of 'no one understands me' rather than physical separation. There is an important need for connectedness for an entrepreneur. The need for connectedness is the subject of this chapter.

'At the end of the day people won't remember what you said or did, they will remember how you made them feel.'
—Maya Angelou

Connectedness is not about social networking or communication skills; it is about building connections that are empathetic, a quality that is essential to building an organizational culture that is *nurturing* and *compassionate*.

Ram, the CEO of a company, had a reputation for being a hard taskmaster. He was an aggressive, no-nonsense person who did not tolerate mediocrity, a go-getter who was totally focused on achieving the goals of the organization. Employees feared him and were under constant pressure to perform to the standards set by Ram. He seldom hesitated in pulling up his colleagues during presentations and meetings. He believed that one should be 100 per cent prepared for any meeting. The business under him had shown tremendous growth, and he was proud of his achievements. Finally, he had to leave the company due to differences of opinion with members of the new board. When employees were queried about this star performer, most of them did not have pleasant things to say. Fig 7.1 captures the importance of feelings in relationships. Just close your eyes and ask yourself about your favourite aunt or uncle during your childhood or about the great moments you spent with your parents. You will quickly realize that the moments where your parents bought you expensive gifts do not perhaps figure on your list. On the other hand, the loving moments that you spent during a walk with them in a garden nearby might rank at the very top. *Feelings* play an important role in establishing connections that are empathetic and nurturing.

Fig 7.1: When Feelings Get Ignored

There is a common misconception that a business organization does not have a place for emotions. If someone expresses his feelings and vulnerability, it is taken to be an undesirable trait. Let us not forget that a business entity is a paper entity that derives its life from the activities of people attached to it. In fact, the culture of an organization is determined by the people populating the organization.

When people are treated as *objects* rather than people who have dreams, desires and feelings, the *heart is at war,* and this does not help fulfil the need for establishing an empathetic connection with another person. Connectedness is a core universal need that makes the entrepreneurial journey less lonely and makes it enriching and more fulfilling.

Connection through Feelings

Most of us are familiar with words such as empathy, nurture, praise, or compassion. The challenge is in understanding these ideas and implementing them in our daily lives. The 'how to do it' takes time and effort.

> Let us take a sample conversation between salesmen A and B:
>
> A: 'I have not been able to close even one lead in the last five days.'
>
> B: 'I feel sad for you.'
>
> A: 'Whatever I do, nothing seems to be working.'
>
> B: 'Do not get dejected so quickly. Maybe you need to practise more. Perhaps, customers will get interested in the product when you focus on customer benefits instead of talking about the product.'
>
> A: 'Okay.'
>
> B: 'How do you think I was able to close leads? Most potential customers did not show interest. I just persevered with a "never give up attitude". I think that worked.'

Do you see what is happening here? Do you think B was empathetic? Was he making a connection to A that provided *support* and *understanding*? Clearly, the intention of B was to share his experiences so that A could take something from it. How do you think A will receive B's advice?

Let us look at a different response:

A: 'I have not been able to close even one lead in the last five days.'
B: 'It must be upsetting not to get the results you wanted.'
A: 'Yes. Whatever I did, well, nothing seemed to work.'
B: 'Hmm...'
A: 'Maybe I give up too quickly.'
B: 'That must be frustrating. I can share my experiences in similar situations. It could be helpful. You can connect to me anytime on this.'
A: 'Sure. That would help.'

Can you see the difference between the first and the second conversation? Do you think B was trying to connect to A in the above instance?

The window of connection to another person is through the heart. A was in need of support and understanding. He seemed upset and frustrated. He was not looking for advice, judgement, philosophical talk, or analysis of any kind. He was just looking for someone who could understand what he was going through. In the first conversation, B was into himself. He made feeble attempts to connect but remained focused on himself. He was sympathetic to A's situation but not empathetic. He was quick to talk about himself and his experiences. A is unlikely to be interested in what B had done. In fact, by pointing out to the need for perseverance and a 'go-getter' attitude, B was perhaps, inadvertently giving the message to A that: 'You are not good enough, I am better than you. Learn from me.'

In the other conversation, B was attempting to be with A in his hour of need. He connected to A by connecting to what he was feeling. He guessed that A was perhaps upset and identified the emotion by giving it a name. He avoided giving unsolicited advice and talking about his experiences when it was not warranted. B provided empathy to A and let him know that he was willing to share his experiences whenever A was ready to listen. The connection made by B provided A the option to strengthen it.

> 'Too often we underestimate the power of a touch, a smile, a kind word, a listening ear, an honest compliment, or the smallest act of caring, all of which have the potential to turn a life around.'
> —Leo Buscaglia

Each situation is an opportunity to connect and empathize. In organizations, people usually connect to the head. They apply logic and analysis with the hope that the other person will understand. Unfortunately, when a person is in an intense emotional state, he is seldom listening to the logic that is thrown at him. We usually choose to ignore the fact that people working in business environments have emotions. Increasingly, organizations realize that this dichotomy of expectations can be addressed by taking a work-life integrated approach where the barriers between work and home are blurred.

Here is another example: Chitra was upset because she got reprimanded by her boss in front of everyone. Below are some of the responses she received from her colleagues:

- 'Chill. I have faced this many times. Just ignore him.'
- 'What happened? Did you do something that upset him?'

- 'He is a jerk. I have seen him do this all the time.'
- 'These things happen in most offices. Just take it in your stride. We need to learn to cope with all kinds of people.'
- 'Whatever he did is for your benefit and growth. You can learn from this experience.'
- 'I think you should take up this matter with his boss.'

Well, if you were a friend, what advice would you have for Chitra?

The responses she received were advice, curiosity, judgements, justification, blame and philosophy. What do you think Chitra needed then? Do you think Chitra was not aware of the various options that her friends were advocating? In this situation, Chitra was upset and needed support and understanding. She did not receive it from her friends. Maybe she was not even listening to what her friends were saying.

How does one make the connection with Chitra? A simple acknowledgement of what she was going through would provide that support. One could respond by saying, 'It must be overwhelming for you right now. Would you like to talk about it?'

Well, empathetic connection is the first step to working towards a solution. Fig 7.2 captures the essence of connecting through feelings. Advice, philosophy, analysis, or judgements play a role only after a rapport has been established. They are not relevant when someone is going through a highly emotional, unresourceful

The emotional states of people are not captured in numbers. If you assume that people are happy just because the business is doing exceedingly well, you need to pause and question your assumptions. It may or may not be true.

state. They do not serve the need for empathy and connection. The exploration of various options to address Chitra's predicament comes later. The focus on solutions without addressing the needs of individuals is unlikely to provide *wholesome solutions*, which cater to the needs of the heart and the head. Even if Chitra completes the assigned work, but with resentment or with a heavy heart, the solution is incomplete. This unmet emotional need is unlikely to be visible in a spreadsheet or an outcome registering mechanism. *The human elements of an outcome are not visible in numbers.* Genuine concern for others and their feelings requires internalization of the idea and propagation of this quality in an organization. These are skills that can be developed through appropriate training programs.

Fig 7.2: Connecting Through Feelings

Most organizations have extensive policies on employee welfare, insurance, medical emergencies and education allowance.

When a colleague is hospitalized, appropriate support is usually extended to the family on various fronts. Office colleagues make adjustments based on the demands of the situation. Do we have to wait for events to happen to extend support and understanding? Providing support through policies, physical spaces or flexible working hours, are environmental methods that help in strengthening systemic support and connection to the material needs of an employee. It is imperative that organizational culture reflects the philosophy of understanding and support. These qualities do not need to be exhibited only in emergency situations. They need to be a part of the DNA of any organizational culture. Language used (verbal and non-verbal) is also an indicator of the level of empathy in an organization.

If the hardware is great, but the software has bugs—the overall system is at best going to be patchy and unwholesome. Empathetic individuals and organizations can read the disturbance in the fabric of connectedness, and this makes them take action to reinforce that connectedness.

Building Empathy

The term empathy is used to describe a wide range of experiences. It is defined as the ability to sense other people's emotions, along with the ability to imagine what someone else might be thinking or feeling. It is about tuning into what, how and why people feel and think the way they do, even if those perspectives are different from yours. Empathy is a powerful tool that can make an uneasy relationship more

'Some people think only intellect counts: knowing how to solve problems, knowing how to get by, knowing how to identify an advantage and seize it. But the functions of intellect are insufficient without courage, love, friendship, compassion and empathy.'
—Dean Koontz

collaborative in nature. It strengthens the emotional bond that allows people to work *with* instead of *against* each other.

Empathy can be confused with being nice, agreeable and making pleasant conversation to please others. That is not true. Empathy can be provided even when there are differing points of view.

David (team leader) and Harish (team member) are part of a team working on a project. David heads the team. They have been facing delivery challenges and are behind schedule. Below is a conversation that takes place between the two.

David: 'I have not seen a team that is so lazy and inefficient. No one seems to be interested in completing the assignment on time. Team members do not support each other and are constantly playing the one-upmanship game.'

Harish: 'We have been doing our best. Three members fell sick and have been on leave for the last week. I have been working hard to ensure that we complete it on time.'

David: 'I do not care if someone is on leave or not. I want the job to be done before the weekend.'

Harish: 'All of us have been working overtime due to lack of resources. It is not as if we are not concerned about delivering on time.'

David: 'Is that so? The three members were absent only in the last few days. The project has been delayed by a month. I am answerable to the customers. It looks like you guys do not care.'

David and Harish got into a heated argument on unsupportive team members, delayed delivery schedules, irresponsible behaviour and work attitudes. David was very sarcastic and Harish was defensive. This conversation was unlikely to help reduce the stress of the team. It was more likely to spoil relationships.

Empathy can be effective even when there is a difference of opinion and when emotions run high. Let us look at it through the empathy lens.

David: 'I have not seen a team that is so lazy and inefficient. No one seems to be interested in completing the product on time. Team members do not support each other and are constantly playing the one-upmanship game.'

Harish: 'You are worried that we would not be able to complete the project on time. You would like team members to be supportive of one another so that we can be more effective.'

David: 'Of course! These delays happen when we work at cross purposes.'

Harish: 'You are thinking that the delay is happening because team members are working at cross purposes and this further worries you. What I have noticed is very different; three members have been ill in the last week and have not been able to come to the office. The rest of us have been working overtime to ensure that work does not get impacted. I see members extending a lot of support to each other. I guess that you are perhaps not aware of these developments. Despite being hospitalized, two members are continuously coordinating with us for work.'

David: 'Is that so? I was not aware, and I hope there is nothing serious. But I also hope the project does not get delayed. Please let me know if you require any resources or other support to ensure we are on track.'

In the above conversation, Harish connected to what David was feeling and thinking. After establishing the connection, he was assertive and provided information to buttress his differing point of view without appearing to be antagonistic or argumentative. When empathy is present, the responses are likely to be more balanced and can help meet mutual objectives.

Both David and Harish are working towards meeting the organization's needs.

Providing empathy does not mean that you need to agree or approve the other person's position. Empathy is just an acknowledgement of the other party's views, admitting its existence without passing judgements about its validity. In the above conversation, despite the fact that Harish did not agree to David's viewpoint, he made it a point to acknowledge and paraphrase what David was thinking and saying. He did not get into an argument with David on the validity of his statements.

People often confuse empathy with sympathy. Sympathy involves reacting to what others are thinking and feeling by putting the speaker first. Sympathetic statements begin with the word 'I' whereas empathetic statements begin with a 'you'. You can also use 'it' instead of 'you', as in 'It must be overwhelming for you right now.' When you offer condolences on someone's death, you are likely to start the message with 'My heartfelt condolences'. This is an expression of sympathy and can be effective, but it does not have the power to change relationships.

Anita and Divya, two friends, met at the park. The conversation that followed is below:

Anita: 'My mother-in-law is terrible. She is constantly finding faults with my cooking, my parenting style, my sense of cleanliness, etc. She also blames me for not looking after her son's health. She is a pain.'

Divya: 'I understand. I have similar problems at home.'

Anita: 'I want to pack her off to my sister-in-law's place, but she refuses to go. It is frustrating to deal with her.'

Divya: 'In fact, I get similar thoughts, but my husband does not support me.'

Anita: 'I have been suffering from severe back pain, and

she does not even enquire about me. She is always talking about her problems.'

Divya: 'I feel bad for you when I hear this. Not sure how you are managing all this stress. I do not think I would be able to do all that you are doing. It requires a lot of patience.'

In the above conversation, Divya is trying to be understanding of Anita's plight by drawing similarities between her experiences and that of Anita's. She wants Anita to know that she is not alone in this journey. Divya also expresses her feelings and attempts to point out Anita's strengths to make her feel better. Is Divya empathetic or sympathetic?

In the above conversation, Divya was trying to be sympathetic. It is unlikely to help in creating a genuine, deep-seated understanding of the other person's situation.

Let us look at an empathetic conversation between the two:

Anita: 'My mother-in-law is terrible. She is constantly picking faults with my cooking, my parenting style, my sense of cleanliness, etc. She also blames me for not looking after her son's health. She is a pain.'

Divya: 'You must be feeling overwhelmed.'

Anita: 'Absolutely. I go through this on a daily basis. I want to pack her off to my sister-in-law's place, but she refuses to go. It is frustrating to deal with her.'

Divya: 'You wish you could send her off for a few weeks so that you can get some rest, peace and time for yourself.'

Anita: 'Exactly. I wish I could do that. I am stressed right now, and I am suffering from severe back pain too.'

Divya: 'I guess you are looking for support and understanding from your mother-in-law. Have you considered taking a break with your husband and going on a holiday?'

Divya is being empathetic to what Anita is going through by using the 'you' language. Using the 'you' language that is not in congruence with non-verbal communication will not work. The tone, gesticulation and the facial expression will reveal if the concern is fake or authentic. Divya built the rapport before providing solutions to the problem.

Other Ways to Connect

There are other ways to establish a connection with people. Dilts's logical levels can help in building such rapports.

Environment: This is the first level of basic connection that one establishes with a group of people. Connecting at this level happens through visible symbols such as the dress that people wear or symbols that represent a common belief system. Symbols are commonplace in religion. Followers of ISKCON have distinctive attire, the Sikhs can be identified by the turban and the five Ks, Christians have the cross and Muslims have the skull cap. These visible symbols help in making an immediate connection with another person.

Building connections at the higher logical levels (Belief, Identity and Spiritual) will make the connection strong and lasting. When you make a connection with your customer at the higher levels, you will notice that brand loyalty improves.

When you walk into a business meeting, it is highly unlikely that you will be dressed in a T-shirt and shorts since it would be incongruous, and you are likely to feel out of place and unwanted by others in the meeting.

Behaviour: The language one speaks, the pace of speech or the amplitude of the voice, can help in establishing the first level of rapport between two people. For instance, if there is congruence between the pace of talk between two people, they will be attracted to each other. If you are someone who speaks fast, you will get bored in the company of people who have a slow and measured way of speaking. The way a person walks (brisk versus slow) or gesticulates, can also be useful in connecting to others.

A connection can happen through shared interests such as hobbies, sports, movies, or music. People with a shared interest in sports and games like to hang out together.

Capability: People who have high levels of professional competency easily connect to others having similar kinds of interests. In fact, if you are good at what you do, people in the same field begin to respect you. They want to hang out with you.

Shared Beliefs and Values: You can establish strong connections through respecting and understanding the beliefs and values of another person even if there is a divergence from your beliefs and values. When you earn the trust and respect of someone else, a bond is created, and the other person will feel safe to share his perspectives on different situations.

Identity: When you begin to respect people for *who they are*, you begin to establish a connection with the individual. Acceptance at this level would entail respect for the core beliefs, values, feelings and actions of the other person. You will then feel comfortable in sharing your core beliefs. If there are hidden agendas, it could lead to manipulations that will break the trust in quick time.

The AAA Model

Shankar, a first generation entrepreneur, aged around forty, is a hardworking, dynamic, action-oriented and a no-nonsense boss. He is a go-getter who likes things to move quickly. He dislikes inaction

Awareness, Acceptance and Action are important elements of the process of change. Without unconditional acceptance, the action would be incomplete and uncomfortable.

and does not tolerate mediocrity. Recently, when he visited his doctor he realized that his blood pressure was 180/120, which is very high. His doctor advised immediate medication and let him know that the high BP was due to stress. Shankar did not believe it and was not willing to accept that he might have to take BP medicines for the rest of his life. He did not have any other illnesses.

'Shankar, the stress you are experiencing is due to work overload. Your body needs some rest,' the doctor told Shankar.

'I do not understand how I can be under stress. I am a happy-go-lucky, hard-working individual like anyone else. I seldom get angry, and neither am I short-tempered. I enjoy life to the fullest. I am not sure if you are right in your assessment, doctor,' replied Shankar.

'Are you constantly thinking about your business?' asked the doctor.

'Yes I am, but nothing that needs to cause any worry. My business requires me to plan for the future, and I am usually busy doing that,' remarked Shankar 'and I ensure that I do not repeat the mistakes of the past.'

'I want you to listen carefully, Shankar. Here is the basic problem. And this happens with most of my patients. Many of them live in denial that they are facing an issue and ignore the need to change themselves in order to lead a life free of potential medical issues in the future. And this happens because of a *lack of awareness* of what they are feeling and the *lack of self-acceptance*,' explained the doctor.

'What does that mean?' asked Shankar.

'Self-awareness is about being present in the moment instead of thinking too much about the past that cannot be changed or thinking too much about the future that is yet to arrive. It is all about *being in the now*, and being able to identify and articulate your feelings. Your feelings are likely to manifest themselves in the body. You are likely to have a tingling sensation, stiffness of the neck, muscles tightening, sweating palms or breathlessness. When this happens, you need to follow strategies to calm your mind and body consciously. Most people are not even aware of their feelings, and this is the first step towards addressing the issue that you're facing,' continued the doctor, 'When the mind is working feverishly in the past and the future, it causes stress due to secretion of neurochemicals in the body. Most of the stress is related to overworked minds.'

'Hmm... I do get bouts of anxiety when I think about the future of the business. What you are saying is true. I might appear calm, but my mind is definitely in an overactive state,' agreed a reflective Shankar.

'The second step is to *accept* that you have a problem. No action will be useful if there is no acceptance that you have an issue on hand. Acceptance would mean that you are not in the denial mode. Once you are aware of what you are feeling, and accept that feeling, you are ready for the third step—action,' explained the doctor.

'Are you referring to the need for connecting with oneself?' asked Shankar.

'Absolutely. In fact, we call this the basic AAA framework of *awareness*, *acceptance* and *action*. To solve an issue, you need to be aware of the issue, be willing to accept the problem and then begin to address the issue,' continued the doctor.

The AAA model is simple and yet very powerful. Becoming self-aware will enable you to catch problems at an early stage before they become monsters. The need to connect to oneself and to become self-aware is an important component of the model that we will cover in the next section, the NVC model.

Communication: The NVC Model

If you observe people communicating, they usually use a language that seeks to get things 'done my way'. There is a need to influence, persuade, negotiate and plead to veer the other person to your point of view at any cost, often ignoring or feigning to understand the other point of view. In TV debates, you will notice that most participants try their best to get their points of views across without actually listening deeply to what others are saying. When there is a hidden agenda, there is an attempt to manipulate the outcome of a conversation, and the lack of authenticity will be clearly visible.

Communication is a mirror that reflects the way we think, our beliefs and our values. It provides an insight into the other person's model of the world. Effective communication is not about *what you say* but about *how the other person receives, interprets and responds*.

'Non-Violent Communication', as propounded by Dr Marshall B. Rosenberg, provides an effective model of communicating with compassion and empathy. Language that we use reflects the way we think and experience the world. There are some forms of language that have a tendency to alienate us from the people around us. NVC identifies four forms of language that can be alienating:

Moralistic Judgements

Moralistic judgements refer to the use of language that implies rightness or wrongness on the part of people whose actions are not aligned with our values. These are judgements that result in blame, insults, put-downs, labels, criticism and comparisons.

For example, 'People around me are useless,' 'It is not right for employees to go on strike,' 'That team member is lazy,' 'My boss is mean and unreasonable', 'That customer is crazy. He is never happy with anything that we sell', 'I have a bunch of people who are good at nothing', 'You are the only one who knows the answer. The rest are fools.' These are judgement statements that imply that there is a *right* and a *wrong* way to do things.

Our analysis of other human beings revolves around classification, evaluation and checking out the level of wrongness rather than on the needs of ours and others. When your boss wants you to work until 6 p.m. every day he is 'mean and unreasonable'. When you choose to work until 6 p.m. every day, you are 'hard working'. When your boss keeps asking you for the nuts and bolts of every transaction, he is 'a pain and overbearing'. When you ask for details, you are 'meticulous and detail-oriented.'

The main issue is that these forms of communication make people either defensive or resistant to the changes that you wish to see in them. On the other hand, if they do change, it could be out of fear, guilt, or shame.

Making Comparisons

One easy way to make yourself feel miserable is to compare yourself with others. And we are not referring to physical attributes; you could take another parameter that is the cornerstone of performance in organizations—achievement. All you need to do is compare yourself with the star performer in your organization or your team, look at TV shows where you will find talented people who have done so much at such a young

'The only time you look in your neighbor's bowl is to make sure that they have enough. You don't look in your neighbor's bowl to see if you have as much as them.'

—Louis C.K.

Fig 7.3: Effect of Comparison

age, read the newspaper to see how people under the age of thirty have made millions, look at how the neighbour's kids are much smarter than your kids in many areas, or attend your school or college alumni function and realize that your classmates earn much more money than you do. Ask yourself, 'How does it feel when I make these comparisons?' These comparisons are likely to make you feel unhappy, heavy-hearted, uncomfortable, jealous, hurtful, insecure, or embarrassed. Comparisons do not help your cause of respecting and accepting yourself the way you are. Instead, they are bound to make you feel miserable.

The sales head makes the following statement in front of salespeople who have gathered for a regular sales review meeting, with the belief that it will motivate others to do as well:

'Rohit is the best salesperson we have, all of you can learn from him.'

How would that make others feel? Would that be motivating? Or would it shift the focus from 'how to improve sales effectiveness' to 'how to become more like Rohit'?

It would add value to other salespeople if the boss focuses on the qualities that helped in improving sales effectiveness. He could rephrase it as:

'Rohit has been closing fifty deals every month during the last three months. We would like to hear from him about his experience.'

The boss is no longer comparing others to Rohit, and the focus of the other salesmen will be on learning from Rohit's experiences while he also gets acknowledged for his achievements.

Denial of Responsibility

This happens when we do not accept responsibility for our actions and attribute the causes to factors outside of ourselves. When we do that, we deny the existence of a choice where we can take ownership of an action. Here are a few statements that highlight denial of responsibility—'I am staying late at the office because my boss asked me to do so,' 'I did not get a bonus because my boss conspired against me,' 'You make me feel sad,' 'I had to come early to office because my boss wanted me to finish the work by 10 a.m.' 'I fell sick because of the weather,' 'I

Denying responsibility for one's actions shifts the locus of control to external forces. This results in blame, criticism and conflict. This will alienate others around and make life less enriching.

bribed the official because he asked me for a bribe,' or 'I could not close the sale because of my incompetent colleagues.' When we do not take ownership for what we feel, think and do, we become unaware of the possibilities that can help us take control of our actions. When you do not take ownership, there is a propensity to blame others. On the contrary, when you accept ownership of your actions it makes you feel powerful, in control of the situation and ready for change.

Fig 7.4: Shifting Responsibility to Others

Let us reframe the above statements with emphasis on choices and ownership:

- I am staying late at the office because my boss asked me to do so.
  I am staying late in the office because I chose to.
- I did not get a bonus because my boss conspired against me.

I did not get a bonus because I did not meet the targets.
- You make me feel sad.
  I choose to feel sad.
- I had to come early to the office because my boss wanted me to finish my work before 10 a.m.
  I chose to come early so that I could finish my work before 10 a.m.
- I fell sick because of the weather.
  I fell sick because I did not look after myself.
- I bribed the official because he asked me for a bribe.
  I chose to bribe the official.
- I could not close the sale because of my incompetent colleagues.
  I could not close the sale. I need to learn and do better next time.

Situations outside of yourself can act as triggers, but your interpretations of these situations are responsible for how you feel, think and behave.

Demands and Requests

When we make demands of others, either explicitly or implicitly, it makes others feel threatened with blame or punishment if they fail to comply. This behaviour does not meet the need for connecting to the other person. This happens where there is a hierarchy of power and authority. The assumption of those in power is that it is their job to change other people and make them behave as per their requirements. The need for control causes resentment, fear and anger. By placing demands on others, those in authority are likely to ensure compliant behaviour. But people should change because they want to, and not out of fear of punishment.

You can know if you are making a demand or a request by observing the response you get.

Boss: 'I would like to have the report on my table by 6 p.m. today.'

Employee: 'I need to leave by 5 p.m. I need to take my son to the doctor.'

Boss: 'Even I have problems at home, but I am still doing my duty. I don't want to hear anything more on this. I want this by 6 p.m.'

The above conversation shows that the first statement is not a request but a demand. The employee is likely to stay behind and do the work out of fear, resentment and helplessness. This does not help the cause of showing compassion or building a connection with the employee. Let us look at the conversation through the lens of compassion:

Boss: 'I would like the report on my table by 6 p.m. today.'

Employee: 'I need to leave by 5 p.m. I need to take my son to the doctor.'

Boss: 'Hmm… I hope there is nothing serious. You seem worried.'

Employee: 'He is suffering from a cold and I had fixed up an appointment for 5.15 p.m. The doctor will not be available after 6 p.m.'

Boss: 'Okay. Would it work if you leave by 4.45 p.m., take your son to the doctor and return to the office by 5.30 p.m.? I will talk to my driver and you can take my car. In fact, I can request an extension of the deadline by a couple of hours. Would that work for you?'

Employee: 'I guess that would be workable. Thanks.'

In this case, the boss made a request, connected to the concerns of the employee, provided an alternative that was workable and earned the goodwill of the employee. I am sure you will agree that this employee will go out of the way to help the boss in the future.

Summary

This chapter dealt with the important topic of connectedness and empathy. The entrepreneurial journey is lonely, and it becomes all the more important for entrepreneurs to become aware of the need for empathy in dealing with people.

We looked at how one can build trusting, nurturing and empathetic connections with others in the organization, how one can build bridges with others by connecting to their hearts. We also explored ways to build rapport with others. The NVC communication model highlighted the four kinds of language that alienates people from one another.

When people are in a highly emotional state, it is important to address the emotional state before getting into the solution mode that addresses the analytical aspects of the situation. Feelings can be used to connect to people using appropriate language. The NVC model provided some clues about usage of language and its consequences.

8

Emotional Intelligence

Arun is a very successful entrepreneur. Rob, a friend of his, noticed something curious about Arun's behaviour. Whenever Arun won contracts that pitted him against stiff competition, it got him excited and charged up. There would be an air of confidence and sure-footedness in his actions. But in the last few months, he had started to lose contracts, employees started quitting, profit margins were getting squeezed, and all through Rob was expecting Arun to be carrying these worries on his shoulders. Rob was pleasantly surprised when he found him to be the same old chirpy bird, full of energy, enthusiasm and positivity. It seemed that the accumulated stress did not impact him in any way. When Rob asked him about it, Arun gave an interesting response, 'What you say is true. There are many events happening around me that can put a person down. When I come across such situations, *I take ownership of what I am feeling* and do not let circumstances dictate my thinking and feelings in a way that would worsen the situation.'

'People's emotions are rarely put into words, far more often they are expressed through other cues. The key to intuiting another's feelings is in the ability to read non-verbal channels, tone of voice, gesture, facial expressions and the like.'
—Daniel Goleman

'Well, what about the highs when you win contracts? Don't you allow circumstances to dictate how you are feeling then?' Rob asked.

'I choose to feel a certain way because it helps me in a given situation. I am aware of the signalling effect of my behaviour on people around me. When I am energetic, confident and motivated, I begin to see the same qualities in others,' he replied.

'But, isn't that faking? Hiding your emotions when it suits you, isn't that being unauthentic?' Rob was left puzzled.

'I look at it like this: circumstances are not responsible for what I think and feel. They could trigger a line of thought, but it is my interpretation of the event that is responsible for the way I feel. If I can catch the thoughts that make me feel depressed or frustrated in a given situation, I can reframe my thoughts and look at it as a learning experience, a lesson that is necessary for the journey of life. It helps to keep me curious, motivated and excited.'

'Easier said than done!' Rob quipped.

'Yes, it takes time and effort. It has taken me years of consciously working on myself to reach the stage where my responses to situations are unconsciously geared towards looking at them as learning experiences. And I am still learning,' explained Arun.

'Are you saying you deny yourself the experience of feeling sad, frustrated and helpless in adverse situations?'

'Well, yes and no. I open myself to various feelings, expose my vulnerability and share my frustrations with my team. I verbalize my thoughts and feelings, but I do not let it impact my behaviour in a way that is not in the interests of my team and the business. In fact, I let everyone know that it is acceptable to express your feelings in the office environment. I believe that bottled up emotions can manifest themselves in undesirable behaviour. I have consciously developed an optimistic view of life that enables me to see all experiences as a necessary learning that is meant to help me grow. I have internalized the reframing process, and it helps my team and me to gear ourselves towards the needs of the business. I call it *needs-oriented* adaptation. I focus on the needs that are required to be met instead of focusing on my interpretation and the resultant behaviour.'

What are Feelings and Emotions?[11]

According to both Carl Jung and the social anthropologist Abner Cohen, objects draw and invoke emotions. This is a natural phenomenon and is essential for human survival. When you encounter an unknown object, you may have a range of sensations, such as curiosity or fear. When you give that unknown a name, it becomes a significant symbol of meaning.

It is through this process that emotions become attached to every object in the universe. When an object is named, it comes to hold a meaning. Emotions are an abstract, metaphysical state of mind. Emotions establish your attitude toward reality and provide your drive for all of the life's pleasures.

Additionally, these emotions are connected to your biological systems and are designed to alert you of danger or to draw you to something pleasurable. If you did not possess emotions, you would carelessly walk right up to a lion in the Savanna wilderness, or if you were starving, you would not have the motivation to climb a tree and pick its fruit to eat.

As the objects in your world produce emotions within you,

---

[11]Source: http://johnvoris.com/featured-articles/difference-between-emotions-and-feelings/

those emotions are collected in the subconscious and begin to accumulate. This is especially true when similar events are repeatedly experienced. Ultimately, they form an emotional conclusion about how to live life and, more importantly, how to survive physically and mentally in a world of chaos. When this happens, a feeling is born. In this way, emotions serve as a kind of 'feelings factory'.

Emotional States and Locus of Control

We often refer to successful ventures in terms of aggregate metrics of measurement such as ratios, margins, growth rates, or return on investments—all of which are aligned with the performance of a business entity. They do not reflect the emotional states of the people behind the metrics. It is assumed that successful business ventures will mean happy and successful promoters and employees. Often, this results in promoters (and employees) increasingly identifying themselves with the performance of their businesses. When the business does well, it is exciting, and when the business does poorly, it is time to mourn and feel depressed. This merging of identities moves the locus of control of emotional states to external factors outside of one's control.

In the earlier example, what Arun did was this: he took ownership of what he was feeling, ensured that the locus of control was with him and not with an external event, reframed his thoughts and adapted to situations, all the while keeping in mind the needs of his organization.

Identifying with Business Performance

When a person begins to equate the performance of the entity with his need for growth, stability and predictability, he is likely to get attached to the experiences of the business entity.

For instance, the thoughts of an employee when the business is going through a rough patch could be, 'Will I get my salary next month? Will I lose my job? What will happen to the promotion that I am expecting? Will I get the increment and bonus this year?' The concern for the business is likely to stem from the anxiety about one's future in the organization. The concerns are very similar for an entrepreneur too. When the business is not doing well, the thoughts could be, 'Why are we not able to grow? Will I be able to retain people? What will happen to our cash position next month? Will I be able to pay for salaries? How do I keep my staff motivated?' These thoughts are likely to make one feel anxious, stressed, frustrated, helpless and perhaps irritated too. There is a high likelihood that these feelings will get transferred to the personal lives of employees. It is important to remember that people have a life beyond business and their role in their workplace is just one part of them.

Have you noticed how you respond to people at home when your organization has been voted as one of the best companies to work for? How will you respond when you hear that your organization has not grown in the last eight quarters whereas your competitors have done exceedingly well? What would be your thoughts in the above two circumstances? How does it impact your behaviour? Would you start applying for jobs elsewhere? Would it impact the way you respond to people at home? How does one ensure that these events do not impact

'75 per cent of careers are derailed for reasons related to emotional competencies, including inability to handle interpersonal problems; unsatisfactory team leadership during times of difficulty or conflict; or inability to adapt to change or elicit trust.'—The centre for Creative Leadership

us and our personal lives in a way that makes it stressful?

Arun reframed the way he interpreted events, and this enabled him to change the way he responded to the situation. This process takes time and practice.

Working with People: Building Emotional Intelligence

In the earlier section, we considered the consequences of identifying one's feelings with the performance of the business. The business entity's performance is an aggregate measurement of all the actions taken and their consequences. The aggregate numbers do not reflect the emotional states of human interactions. The stimulus and response loop of human interactions are likely to invoke many emotions in the people participating in these interactions. What is the impact on emotional states when people interact? What is emotional intelligence (EI) and how do you develop it?

Peter Salovey and Jack Mayer, who created the term emotional intelligence, describe it as:

> [The] ability to perceive emotions, to access and generate emotions so as to assist thought, to understand emotions and emotional meanings, and to reflectively regulate emotions in ways that promote emotional and intellectual growth.

In other words, it is the common sense that we often refer to; that helps us navigate the world, be sensitive to the needs of others and develop social skills of survival.

Emotions get generated when we begin to interpret the world around us and they get manifested physiologically in our body as sensations. For example, if you were to see a snake on the ground, and if your interpretation of a snake is that 'all snakes are poisonous and can kill in minutes,' you are likely to get scared. This emotion is likely to manifest itself in your body through stiffening of your calf muscles, heavy breathing and sweating. You are likely to respond by either running from the scene or being transfixed and numbed into inaction. We have effectively attached the emotion 'scared' to the object called 'snake'.

The same logic applies when we interact with people. Some emotions like anger, depression, stress, panic, rage, or despair can be alienating. These emotions can manifest themselves with undesirable consequences that can cause considerable damage to relationships.

Ashok is one of the co-founders of a start-up, which is going through a challenging phase. The week before, he had made a pitch to one of the clients and the client had asked some technical software-related questions that Ashok was not able to answer convincingly. He could not close the sale. For the next meeting, he decided to take Gautam, the technology co-founder, to the presentation. Gautam confirmed that he would come for the meeting, and he was scheduled to join Ashok at their office so that they could go together. But he did not turn up and was not picking up the calls either. Ashok was heard shouting before the staff: 'People around me are useless. I have to deal with such irresponsible behaviour!' After waiting for twenty minutes, Ashok left for the meeting in a huff, all alone. He was irritated and angry. And the important presentation did not go well, despite the fact that there were no deep technical queries from the potential customer.

When you become aware of the triggers that make you angry, stressed or frustrated, you can examine your beliefs about those triggers, and check for alternate interpretations that will help you change your emotional state.

The business lost a potential sale. Also, the seeds of distrust were sown between the co-founders, and this was likely to impact the morale of the office staff adversely. What do you think happened? Ashok did not have full awareness of his emotions, awareness of the cause of his emotions, their impact on his behaviour, and the consequences of his behaviour on the people and events around him. He did not realize that his anger had nothing to do with Gautam. Instead, it had more to do with his frustrations about not being able to get orders and the general state of the business. He did not think twice before blurting out unpleasant words about his co-founder before the whole office.

Could he have handled it differently? Below is the same Ashok doing that.

Soon after Gautam did not turn up or return his calls, an anxious Ashok said to a colleague, 'I am worried. This is very unlike him. I hope he is not in trouble. Please keep me posted if you hear from him.' And to himself he muttered, 'I will have to manage on my own. I was upset last time because I could not answer the customer's queries and that resulted in losing the deal. If there are technical queries, I will ask for time and come back to the customer later. I have managed situations like this before, and I think I can manage this one too.' As soon as his meeting ended, he called up the office to check if they had heard from Gautam. He learnt that Gautam had to rush his father to hospital and had forgotten to carry his mobile phone. Gautam had called Ashok, but Ashok's mobile phone was switched off as he was in the midst of the presentation.

In the second instance, Ashok was aware of his feelings, reflected on his experience and was genuinely concerned for his colleague. He had a strategy in place to manage the situation. In the process, he also won the respect of his office staff for his empathy and understanding. He exhibited emotional intelligence.

Such incidents are very common, and when these misunderstandings pile up, the start-up begins to break from the top. Sometimes, the person may not verbalize his opinion in front of the staff like Ashok did. But even if the thought gets embedded in Ashok's mind, it is equally detrimental. So, what can we do to develop emotional intelligence?

Emotional Self-Awareness

Building emotional intelligence (EI) starts with self-awareness. EI is the ability to recognize your feelings, to differentiate between them, to know the causes of these feelings and to become aware of the impact of your feelings on others.

In the earlier example, Ashok was unaware of how his feelings and behaviour was undermining his effectiveness at an important business presentation. Let us extend the illustrated example. Ashok had come to realize that he lost the important sales account due to his inability to provide satisfactory solutions during the sales pitch. He went home and saw shoes, socks, a school bag and uniform strewn around the living room. He saw Varun, his ten-year-old son, sitting at the dining table and playing a video game.

'Hi, Dad!' greeted Varun, running towards his father to hug him.

'What is all this?' Ashok exclaimed, pointing to the shoes, socks and clothes strewn around the room.

'Is this the place for keeping your shoes? How many times do I have to tell you that shoes are to be kept in the rack? You are no longer a child,' he remarked with irritation writ all over his face.

'Okay, Dad. You don't have to keep repeating it. I have

just come back from school, and I will clean it up after I have my food,' replied Varun.

Fig 8.1: How Business Performance Can Affect Emotional States

'And what is this? What is the video game doing on the dining table? I made a big mistake buying this for an irresponsible child like you. No more video games for a week,' continued an angry Ashok.

'That's not fair. I was waiting for Mummy to get my food and thought I would play a game until then,' replied Varun 'and I did not switch on the TV.'

Divya, Ashok's wife, heard the commotion in the living room and walked in from the kitchen. 'What is going on here?' She realized that something was not quite right. 'Ashok, you look tired and irritated. What happened? Shall I get you a nice, hot coffee?'

'Look at the mess in the house. I have told you many times not to let Varun play video games all the time. When is he going to learn that he must keep the shoes in the shoe rack?'

'He is just a child. He will learn. I had given him permission to play for twenty minutes while I prepared his food,' Divya responded.

'It is entirely your fault. I do not know what happens at home when I am in office. It is your responsibility to bring up the children properly,' replied Ashok in a high pitched tone. He was still irritated.

'What do you mean it is my responsibility? It is yours as well! I do a lot of work at home, and I get tired by the end of day. You always put me down by saying things like this,' replied a visibly upset Divya.

I'm sure you can imagine how this conversation proceeded. The problems at the office spilled over into the personal domain. Ashok, the brilliant business strategist, is the same Ashok at home too. His behaviour towards the events at home and at the office are likely to cause irreparable damage to relationships. The point is simple: if you are not emotionally aware, you are likely to have a dysfunctional life that alienates people.

Emotional awareness is the first necessary step to building emotional intelligence. How can you change something when you are not even aware of it? Mastering this skill will empower you to improve your quality of life.

Reframing Perception: ABCDE Model

The ABCDE model for altering your perception, attitudes and behaviour was pioneered by Dr Albert Ellis, the father of Rational Emotive Behaviour Theory. The core takeaway is that you can change your feelings through logical and deductive reasoning. Let us take Ashok's case and apply the ABCDE model to it.

Ashok was upset with Gautam because he did not turn

up to join an important business meeting. In the ABCDE model, Gautam's failure to turn up for the meeting is called the Activating Agent (A), and Ashok's reaction is called the Consequence (C). Ashok felt angry, frustrated and upset. He verbalized his feelings by blaming, generalizing and judging people around him. But did (A) cause (C)? Well, (A) could have triggered a reaction but what caused (C) was the interpretation that Ashok gave to the event (A). This was based on his Beliefs (B). These beliefs are nothing but thoughts and assumptions that have been reinforced over a period until they have become truths for him. Beliefs manifest as 'self-talk' (or inner dialogue). If Ashok can change his (B) and replace it with beliefs that are life enriching, he can have a consequence that improves his emotional intelligence, rather than alienating the people around him. One can refer to changing (B) as 'reframing'. Connecting to the (B) is at the core of this model, as this enables you to change or reframe your beliefs, and thus change your feelings and behaviour.

Now that we know what (A), (B) and (C) mean, let us fill in the ABCDE chart below (from Ashok's point of view):

Step 1: Let us fill column C with the unpleasant feelings and behaviour that Ashok experienced.

A	B	C
		I feel angry, frustrated, upset and agitated. I am restless. I blame people around me and call them useless and irresponsible.

Step 2: Fill column A with details of the activating agent (the trigger) without passing judgements. Fill in observations only.

A	B	C
Gautam did not turn up at the office and did not call either. I tried calling his number many times but no one is picking up.		I feel angry, frustrated, upset and agitated. I am restless. I blame people around me and call them useless and irresponsible.

Step 3: Fill column B with your beliefs and the interpretation that you have given to the trigger. These are the thoughts that came to you soon after the trigger event happened.

A	B	C
Gautam did not turn up at the office and did not call either. I tried calling his number many times but no one is picking up.	Gautam knows how important this meeting is for us and it is irresponsible of him not to come. He is deliberately avoiding me and my calls. He wants to see to it that I do not do well so that he can blame me for the business not doing well. Since he handles the IT portfolio, he thinks marketing meetings are not his core responsibility. Everyone around me is insincere and incompetent. Nothing is working for me. I am the only one who is working so hard.	I feel angry, frustrated, upset and agitated. I am restless. I blame people around me and call them useless and irresponsible.

The next task is to Debate, Dispute and Discard (D) these self-defeating and maladaptive thoughts that have given rise to the Cs. This is done by logically asking questions such as:

- What is the evidence that supports or does not support your interpretation?
- Are there other logical explanations to explain the activating event?
- If someone asked me for advice about this event, what could I tell them that would help change his or her perspective?
- How would someone whose opinion you (role model) respect respond to my interpretations?
- Have I faced similar situations earlier where my interpretations were proved wrong?
- If yes, did I learn anything that I can apply to the present situation?

Step 4: Fill column D with your responses to the thoughts you have listed in column B by asking the above questions.

A	B	C	D
Gautam did not turn up at the office and did not call either. I tried calling his number many times, but no one is picking up the call.	It is irresponsible of him not to come for the meeting. People should come to meetings on time.	I feel angry, frustrated, upset and agitated. I am restless. I blame people around me and call them useless and irresponsible.	He has seldom missed any meeting in the past.
	He must be deliberately avoiding me and my calls.		If he can't make it, he always calls up.

	He should have at least called.		I have been meeting him every day to discuss some issues.
	He wants to see to it that I do not do well so that he can blame me for the business not doing well.		I have not heard him blame me for any shortcomings in closing sales calls.
	Since he handles the IT portfolio, he thinks marketing meetings are not his core responsibility.		He has taken up responsibility for managing accounts, which is not his core responsibility.
	Everyone around me is insincere and incompetent.		It is possible that he is not picking up calls because his mobile phone is not with him.
	Nothing is working for me.		Some emergency must have cropped up.
	I must be the only one who is working so hard.		'Chill Ashok. You are overreacting. Learn to handle such exigencies.'

			Have you considered the fact that he could be in some trouble?
			I have also been late for many meetings in the past, and I do not think I am irresponsible.
			I would not like to be called useless.
			What I am today is because of the help from my office staff and others.
			I need to work on the way I react to situations.

Step 5: Write down the impact of the debating, disputing and discarding exercises you did in column D and how it has changed that way you look at the activating event, your feelings and behaviour. Column E (E stands for the Effects of changing your interpretation) is not shown in the table, and you can fill it in yourself.

The power of the ABCDE model lies in the fact that through appropriate questioning, you can change your illogical and maladaptive beliefs to logical and adaptive beliefs that will result in adaptive feelings and behaviour.

When there is 'must' and 'should' in the way we think about the world, it raises certain demands and expectations from ourselves and others. These are one's interpretations and have no universal validity. When such individual beliefs are unfulfilled, it gives rise to feelings of anger, rage, despair, depression, pessimism and fear. When Ashok thinks that 'people *should* come to meetings on time', one could ask 'what would happen if someone were to come five minutes late?' If Ashok changes his 'should' to 'prefer', it will provide a more flexible and calmer environment where extreme feelings can be avoided. This does not in any way mean that Ashok cannot express his opinion. He can be assertive and let others know that punctuality meets his need for structure and respect for another person's time.

Managing Stress

The word 'stress' has its origins in physics. It refers to the mechanical force that acts on a body. The reaction to this stress is called strain. In the context of humans, a threatening situation results in a physiological response that prepares us to either 'fight or take flight.' In response to danger, body muscles stiffen, facial expressions change and you get goosebumps. These responses are usually reflex and are not a conscious effort made by us. When the mind and the body react in ways to increase stress, it can result in fear, anxiety, depression, insomnia and physical symptoms such as high BP, chest pains, or shortness of breath. By consciously working on the way we think about events, we can manage how we feel and respond to situations.

> 'Stress is caused by being "here" but wanting to be "there".'
> —Eckhart Tolle

Building emotional intelligence and working on reframing

thoughts using the ABCDE model can help in coping with stress. Managing stress means remaining calm in the face of trying circumstances without getting carried away by intense emotions. It also requires having a sense of control or influence over the events that are triggering the stress, taking appropriate action to limit the consequences of stress, avoiding panic reactions, chunking the problem into manageable parts and being optimistic in the event of negative experiences.

M.S. Dhoni, former Indian cricket team captain, was often called 'captain cool' for his ability to remain calm and composed under all circumstances. He exhibited high levels of emotional intelligence, managed to keep his emotions in check, made logical decisions and provided effective leadership to the team. He maintains equanimity during success and failure, does not lash out at his team in public, is adept at handling criticism or praise and commands the respect of his teammates.

Fig 8.2: Reframing the Way One Thinks About a Situation

There can be an adverse impact on the family if a person is not able to develop emotional intelligence. Sunita is a thirty-eight-year-old woman facing multiple challenges at home. She has two kids aged ten and twelve. She relocated with her family to India a few years ago because her highly qualified husband lost his job in the US. He was doing small assignments but did not have a steady job. After relocating to India, her husband again could not find a suitable job, began to doubt his capabilities, developed low self-esteem, was depressed, and began drinking regularly. In fact, he became an alcoholic and had to be admitted to a rehab for treatment. The family was low on savings, did not have a house of their own and had to shift from a comfortable 3-BHK rented house to a 1-BHK one. This transition had a huge impact on the kids. They were going through emotional turmoil, and this was impacting their performance at school. Sunita's aging mom, a pensioner, stays with her and provides financial support. Sunita took up a job for ₹15,000 per month as a teacher in a school and had to run the family within this budget. She was completely stressed out at school, was overwhelmed with the responsibility of looking after the needs of her children and mom and her own emotional needs. The world appeared to be breaking apart for her. The family that was once doing very well seemed to be going through hell. She was feeling helpless, frustrated, angry, irritated and anxious and these feelings manifested themselves in the form of lack of sleep, constant headaches, body pains, stiff shoulders and neck, and shortness of breath. Her thoughts were: 'Why is this happening to me? I can't bear this anymore. How am I going to bring up the kids? Nobody cares. Is there someone who could help us?'

She would always have a distant look on her face: her facial expressions displayed immense sadness, her drooping shoulders displayed tiredness, and she became increasingly irritated with the children. She was unable to afford basic luxuries, felt guilty and cried in silence. She started medication for her rising BP. How can she manage her stress levels? Where is she going to find the strength to manage herself and the family?

The ABCDE model provides insight into what can help her manage her stress levels. Developing emotional intelligence can help her and her children:

Step 1: Sunita needs to become emotionally self-aware about her thoughts (negative self-talk), feelings and behaviour. She needs to continue to look after her physical health by continuing the medication for BP and making regular visits to the doctor.

Step 2: Catch the self-talk and reframe it. It becomes important to develop an optimistic view. Reframing thoughts:

- 'I have lost everything' to 'I still have something. I have a family and two lovely children. I have a supportive mother.'
- 'Why should this happen only to us?' to 'Everything happens for a reason. This situation is meant to be a learning lesson and is teaching us to be grateful for what we have. This is a phase in life, and we will get over this.'
- 'Despite knowing our present condition, the children continue to be unreasonable. They know mummy is working so hard and is having a tough time. They just don't seem to understand!' to 'My children are going through a tough time themselves and need security, stability, love and emotional support. I need to be more understanding.'
- 'Nobody cares. I have no friends, and I cannot talk

about my personal challenges with everyone' to 'There are people who can help. I could seek the support of a counsellor or a mentor who can help me get more clarity in life. Let me not hesitate to contact people for help.'

- 'My husband is a loser. He is responsible for our condition' to 'We have had great times and he has been caring and affectionate in the past. He has not been able to manage himself, and he is low on confidence. I am doing my best to extend all help so that we can get back to a normal life again.'

- 'My children are suffering because we do not have money, and it makes me feel very angry' to 'My children will learn to cope with difficulties. This situation is a lesson that will make them stronger. I need to be positive and avoid passing negative vibes to my kids. I am grateful that my children are at least healthy.'

- 'The pressure at the school is very high. I have been given additional responsibilities for the next month' to 'The sky is not going to fall if I refuse the additional responsibility. I will talk to my colleagues and see if they can help to take over this responsibility.'

Sunita can become aware of the activating agents (the 'A' in the ABCDE model) in different situations that trigger strong emotions, thoughts and behaviour, analyse if there is a commonality between these triggers, become aware of her beliefs about these triggers, reframe the self-talk and replace the old beliefs with her new interpretations.

Step 3: Evolve strategies to address stressful situations. A few useful tips follow:

- Taking deep breaths can regulate the flow of oxygen in the body and can help in relaxing the mind and body.
- Meditate for twenty minutes in the early morning and at night every day.
- Count slowly to ten.
- Go for a walk.
- Doing exercise or yoga every day.
- Make a plan to chunk down the problem so that it is manageable.
- Talk to a friend or a mentor.
- Listen to soothing music.
- Visualize pleasant images such as a tranquil lake, lots of greenery, or beautiful snow-capped mountains.

Step 4: Set priorities on various issues facing the family, chunk it down so that it is not overwhelming and begin to focus on what is doable.

Summarizing Reframing

Below is a summary of the steps involved in reframing thoughts.

Awareness of Feelings: The first step is to become aware of your feelings, for example, anxiety, fear, anger, frustration, and be able to differentiate one feeling from another. A brief list of feelings is provided in the appendix. Feelings are likely to manifest in your body in some way such as sweating, rapid breathing, cold hands, the stiffness of the muscles in the neck and shoulders and restlessness. You can tune into what your body is telling you.

Awareness of Thoughts: Thoughts are fleeting. However, if you are mindful, you can become aware of the self-talk or inner dialogue that we do throughout the day. Some of these thoughts could be unconscious activity, and you would have to bring them to your conscious state of awareness to catch them. If you can catch the thoughts that are stressing you out, you can question them.

Questioning Thoughts and Beliefs: Questioning enables you to reframe your thoughts. If you are thinking, 'I am going to lose my job,' you can challenge your thinking by asking for evidence: 'What makes you think so? Is it possible that you will not lose your job? Have people retained their jobs in similar situations earlier?' This question will provide you with a wider variety of choices.

Reframing: Once you list down your limiting beliefs and question the logic behind their conclusions, it is time to generate alternate perspectives of the same triggering event. These alternatives will help you *meet your need for an adaptive and an enriching life.*

Summary

Both entrepreneurs and employees need emotional intelligence. Often, events impacting business performance begin to affect the emotional states of people working in the organization. This ensures that the locus of control of one's emotional state remains outside of one's control. The lack of control over one's own emotions begins to have an impact on people's personal lives.

In this chapter, we looked at two broad scenarios—how business performance can impact emotional states, and how events involving people can impact the emotional states of others in the organization. We defined emotional intelligence and showed how it could improve the quality of life at home and the business place.

We applied the ABCDE model of Dr Albert Ellis to explore

ways to replace limiting beliefs with beliefs that are logical, adaptive and life-enriching. This is also called reframing.

Any reframing exercise broadly covers the following steps:

- Awareness of feelings
- Awareness of thoughts
- Questioning thoughts

Doing this will help generate alternate ways of looking at any event.

One of the ways to manage emotions is through logical and deductive reasoning. Words have an impact on the way one experiences the world and developing skills of asking appropriate questions can help a person manage his or her emotions.

9

Coping with Business Failures: The Dark Side of Entrepreneurship

Around five years ago, I received the shocking news of the demise of one of my seniors from college. He was just forty-four years old. He had taken his life due to business-related challenges. He was a professional manager who, along with a few employees, had taken over a business unit from the employer through an 'Employee Buy Out' scheme, with the belief that they could turn around the business. The business manufactured moulded plastic components for various industries in India. However, they faced constant working capital issues and mounting debt, and my friend, who was the CEO, was totally lost and thought the world was closing in on him. Employees had not been taking any salary for many months, and he had a family of three to support (a wife and two young children). Personal finances went dry.

None of his friends or family members knew what was going on with him. He did not speak about his problems to anyone and the stress accumulated inside his head until he couldn't take it anymore.

The dark side of entrepreneurship is seldom spoken about, nor is sufficient emphasis laid on dealing with unexpected adverse outcomes. We often read that only 10 per cent of funded ventures become successful. The majority of them are on the dark side. When business failures are discussed, it is more often in terms of 'analysing why businesses fail' or 'what can we learn from failed ventures'. We see lots of analysis using spreadsheets, financial statements, etc. Everything revolves around measurements and numbers associated with a paper business entity. It is rare to come across any serious reflection about the people involved and how they are coping with disappointments.

Fig 9.1: Taking Failure Personally

Fig 9.1 captures the impact of failures on the psyche of an entrepreneur. The recent case of Angad Paul, Mr Swaraj Paul's son, is a case in point. Angad, the forty-five-year-old CEO of the Caparo group that was founded by his father, suffered massive injuries after he jumped from an eight-storeyed-property in November 2015. He committed suicide. Caparo Industries was facing a crisis due to a collapse in steel prices, forcing sixteen of its companies to be put into administration, a process that is an alternative to liquidation. He took his life despite having the best of education (from MIT) and leading a business worth $1.5 billion. The reason—*unable to cope with business failures.*

For entrepreneurs, business failure is more common than success. Analysing the reasons for business failures happens only after someone has learnt to cope with these failures. This chapter is about how entrepreneurs can read signs of failures, cope with failures, build resilience, and get out of the muck.

What is the Person Thinking?

It requires courage, conviction, perseverance, passion and self-belief to get into entrepreneurship. When the entrepreneur faces his first few obstacles, the usual response is—'These things happen. I will get over it.' The person then works even harder to find solutions to business problems.

> 'I've missed more than 9,000 shots in my career. I've lost almost 300 games. 26 times I've been trusted to take the game winning shot and missed. I've failed over and over and over again in my life. And that is why I succeed.'
> —Michael Jordan

Well, entrepreneurship can be a lonely journey. When the failures start mounting, it becomes unsettling and begins to erode the confidence of the person. Some of the likely thoughts are as follows:

- Maybe there is something wrong with me.
- What will others think of me if they know that my business failed?
- I have disappointed others who placed their faith in me.

- I am not good enough. It is impossible to get this done.
- The universe is against me. Whatever I do is not working.
- Why me?
- This is a dumb world. They don't deserve this product.
- This is getting too much. Maybe I am not fit for this. Let me quit.
- There is no one to talk to. No one will understand what I am going through.
- I am worthless.

What is the Person Feeling?

Failures can invoke intense feelings such as frustration, depression, irritation, stress, sadness, discouragement, helplessness, anger, jealousy, etc. These feelings get manifested in the body through sensations such as heaviness in the heart, increase in body weight, frequent headaches, gastric problems, high blood pressure, breathlessness and drooping shoulders. Self-awareness is a key to coping with the feelings that one goes through. Connecting to oneself by becoming aware of the bodily manifestations of these emotions, accepting the feelings without passing judgements and being aware of their causes will enable you to address the issue. Meditation and breathing are powerful and yet simple techniques that can help a person cope with these emotions.

How is the Person Behaving?

When a person is going through strong emotions, it impacts the way the person responds to others. There could be irritation in the voice, sarcastic language being used, display of reclusive behaviour, and at times, violent behaviour at home and office. Behaviour is the manifestation of how one thinks and feels.

When the chips are down, people respond differently—they get into a cocoon, do not feel like meeting friends, avoid socializing, become irritable, pass sarcastic remarks and put others down. There are some who express their frustration to people around them through violent verbal and non-verbal behaviour.

Ram started a software business with his partner Suresh a few years ago. Ram was the software geek, and Suresh looked after finance and marketing. Since finance was not the domain of Ram, Suresh seldom shared details about financial transactions or the cash position of the company. And for his part, Ram did not show any interest in knowing about the financial health of the firm either. After four years of operations, Suresh let Ram know that there was no money in the firm's bank account. The lack of funds in the bank account surprised Ram as he knew they were doing reasonably well. He quietly downloaded the bank statements and realized that there were many large cash withdrawals and Suresh could not account for these withdrawals. This resulted in a huge showdown between the founders. It was evident to Ram that Suresh had withdrawn money for his personal use without informing him. There was a communication breakdown between the founders. After a few months, Suresh said he was leaving the firm as it was not doing well. Ram felt depressed, frustrated, devastated and helpless. He went into a cocoon. He could not muster the strength to talk about this with his wife or friends. He began to suspect people around him and found it difficult to trust others. He became more short-tempered, and this began to impact his relationship with his wife and kids. Ram began to think that he was a failure.

There are many instances of business failures that can be attributed to the violation of trust between founders.

Coping Strategies

It is imperative that the entrepreneur develops coping strategies. Here are some coping strategies that can help:

- *Just talk*: Talk to someone who is non-judgemental and empathetic. Someone that you are comfortable sharing your fears and dreams. This could be a counsellor, mentor, coach, or trusted friend. It is important to reach out since this is the time when the entrepreneur is likely to retreat into a shell.
- *Self-awareness*: Practise self-awareness exercises (could be meditation or yoga or breathing exercises) to relax your stressed out body and mind.
- *Physical Activity*: Reduce stress through physical activities such as exercising, doing workouts, going for walks, dancing and playing games.
- *Take ownership*: Take responsibility for your choices, thoughts and actions. Giving the control of how you think and feel to external forces such as markets, customers, or teammates is not going to help your cause.
- *Get spiritual*: A trip to a church, mosque, temple, or a spiritual master can be a liberating experience. It will enable one to get grounded in reality and develop different perspectives to one's problems.
- *Reframe thoughts*: When you put yourself down, catch those thoughts and reframe them. One way to catch these fleeting thoughts is to become aware of the *self-talk* that happens in your head. Write it down, if it helps.

Some examples of reframed thoughts are given below:

Failure: I am a failure.

Failure is an unexpected outcome. It is not a personal failure and does not reflect who I am. Failures are experiences of life that will help in building a balanced view of things.

Comparison: I am not good enough. Look at John. He is not as good as I am but he is doing exceedingly well in his career.

I accept the way I am, and I unconditionally accept others for who they are. I will learn from others. There is no room for comparison.

Attitude: These things won't work. I know it.

This is an interesting perspective that I overlooked. What can I learn from it?

Worthiness: I have not achieved anything worth mentioning. I am not good enough.

I am grateful that I have a working brain and a fit body. I am proud of the fact that I made an attempt at entrepreneurship. These bumps do not determine life; it goes beyond business.

Guilt: I regret getting into business. I lost lots of money and precious time that I could have put to better use.

I am thankful that I had an opportunity to try out new things, discover a new me and learn from these experiences.

Family: My friends and customers no longer have confidence in me. No one in the world understands me.

My family has placed their faith in me—unconditionally. What more could I possibly ask for.

Acceptance: This idea has been my baby. Unfortunately, it has not been profitable in the last three years. My family is going through hard times, but I will not give up.

I accept that things have not worked out. It is time to move on. I did my best and I learnt a lot from my experiences. It is time to work on my plan B.

Network: No one cares about me. Others have their problems, and I do not want to trouble them with my issues.

People around me will be happy to help if I ask them. Let me not feel shy about 'asking'.

In the moment: What will people think of me if I quit my business mid-way? What will happen to my employees if I close the business?

Every individual is capable of making his or her decisions. What is the current situation and what can I do right now to meet my needs?

How to Build Resilience?

Resilience gets tested when things do not go your way. When everything is hunky-dory, you are seldom tested. Resilience is an attitude of looking at the positives rather than the negatives, learning from experiences and moving on. It is the ability to bounce back from adversity, difficult situations and failures (in personal and professional life), and to rebuild one's life with renewed vigour and energy. This does not mean that the person is not going to experience emotional distress. Resilience is a skill that can be learnt. It means being adaptable in maintaining balance in life. One of the important factors that contribute to building resilience is having loving, trusting, nurturing and supportive relationships with people around

> 'Resilience is accepting your new reality, even if it's less good than the one you had before. You can fight it, you can do nothing but scream about what you've lost, or you can accept that and try to put together something that's good.'
> — Elizabeth Edwards

you, with both family and non-family members.

Some of the steps associated with building resilience are:

Building Connections: Having healthy relationships with family members and friends is important. Asking and providing support without any pre-conditions and accepting help from people who genuinely care for your well-being strengthens resilience. Some people join various interest groups (Rotary Club, NGOs, etc.) where members support each other.

Reframing: This has been detailed in earlier chapters. You can train yourself to interpret failures and problems as experiences from which you can learn. Look at the positive takeaways that can help you plan and build a better future. Accepting the present situation without constantly focusing on the ifs and buts will help you move forward.

Goal-Setting: Having realistic goals will enable you to focus your energies on something you want for yourself. It is important to enjoy the process. What is important is not the goal in itself but what you become when you achieve your goals.

Taking Action: When the going gets tough, it may require you to make decisions that could have undesirable consequences. Instead of wishing that the problems would just go away, take them on and address the issues proactively.

Personal Growth: Even in adversity, you are likely to have grown and matured in some respect. There are great things to learn from adversity too. In fact, many people who experience tragedies and hardships are in a position to empathize, appreciate relationships, develop a broader perspective of life (spiritually), exhibit resilience and develop enhanced self-worth.

Attitude: The ability to see the bright side of difficult situations can help develop confidence and trust in one's abilities. This also means developing an optimistic outlook and hoping for a better future. It is important to focus on what you want rather than worry about your fears.

Well-being: It is important to take care of your physical and mental well-being. Playing sports, games, or indulging in your hobbies can be fun and relaxing. Meditation can help calm the mind and get you in touch with your needs and feelings.

Building an Optimistic Attitude

The ability to look at the brighter side of things even when faced with adverse conditions helps build an optimistic outlook on life. It assumes that there is hope and this results in a positive approach that is life-enriching.

Sarah had attended more than ten job interviews over the last couple of months but was constantly rejected. She was feeling low and began to lose confidence in herself. She began to think that she was a failure and that there was something wrong with her. She was desperate for a job, as she was a single mother. She had been out of a job for three months now, and her finances were drying up. Her shoulders started to droop, and her body language reflected helplessness and anxiety. She was in tears all the time. Her twelve-year-old daughter, Anna, was aware of the issues that her mother was facing and said to her, 'Mummy! You are the best mom in the world, and I would not trade you for anyone else. This is just a phase, and it will pass. I am sure you have

> 'A pessimist sees the difficulty in every opportunity; an optimist sees the opportunity in every difficulty.'—Winston S. Churchill

also learnt a lot by attending these interviews, and you will clear the next job interview.'

Sarah learnt a lesson about being positive and hopeful, even in adverse situations, from her child. Well, she did not land a job with the next interview, but that lesson helped her see the bright side and be hopeful for the future.

Optimism is not about being foolhardy or unrealistic. It is also not about bombarding yourself with self-talk that repeats positive things about yourself. It is not about putting on rose-tinted glasses and being unrealistic. Reality testing is an important component of being optimistic. Optimism is the ability to stop thinking or saying negative things about yourself and the world around you when you are facing personal setbacks. The following three attitudes help the cause of being optimistic:

- Treating setbacks as temporary phases in life and looking at these setbacks as learning experiences. Setbacks are not permanent.
- Any setback is situational and specific. It is not all pervasive. It is not something that will happen in all contexts and situations. This helps in addressing the specific issue at hand.
- Not to take failure personally, put yourself down or get into self-blame.

Martin Seligman, a psychologist, has provided details of various research studies that show that optimistic people live longer, have fewer illnesses and have a healthy blood pressure.

Signs of Failing and Attempts at Revival

How does one know that the business is on the course downwards? There is a phase lag between the onset of failure and the actual failure happening. Key indicators that can help in discerning the trend are given below:

- Sales growth
- Customer base growth
- Repeat sales

The above key indicators provide insights into the way your product is doing vis-à-vis the competition, how customers perceive your brand, and how you are performing in creating new customers and retaining existing ones. Fig 9.2 captures the dilemma for the entrepreneur. Is the business growing or failing? How does one interpret the signs?

How about other indicators such as cash flows, net margins, industry related issues, market share, etc.? In this context, it must be remembered that the *purpose* of any business is to *create and retain customers*. If you can do just that, you are 'on track'. Repeat sales are an important indicator of the faith reposed by the customer in your brand. Loyal customers provide you with the opportunity to deepen customer relationships.

Challenges such as cash flows, low net margins or people-related issues, can derail a business, but they can also be resolved by taking appropriate actions. Industry-related issues are bound to impact all businesses in the market and are not in your control.

The key word is 'growth' and not just 'sales'. This implies momentum or rate of growth. When sales are stagnant, and customers are not being added and there is no deepening of relationships through repeat sales, it does not augur well. It is a sign to sit up and take action. For instance, when companies pursue an increase in sales by adding new customers but ignore servicing their existing customers, it is unlikely that repeat sales will happen. Also, the important metric to track is not the addition of new customers but the net accretion of customers. This will include dissatisfied customers who have moved on.

Fig 9.2: Different Perceptions About Business Performance

The reasons for these three key indicators dipping could be:

- Building a product that your customer does not want.
- Customer has better options from competitors.
- Poor customer tracking and servicing.
- Ineffective sales planning and strategy.
- Inability to close sales.
- Change in the environment (legal, economic conditions, inflation, etc.).

The above reasons could be related to skills, people, technical and operational issues, a faulty product, stiff competition, or environmental variables. Some of these problems are in your control, but some of them are not. It is important not to get obsessed with competition and to be totally focused on the customer. There are companies that waste too much of energy on tracking competition, getting obsessed even, instead of deploying resources to create and service customers. Competition is pretty much a part of the industry structure, but it cannot be the focus of operations at the expense of meeting the core needs of the organization.

J.K. Rowling: Success After Many Failures

One of the biggest rags-to-riches stories of successful people who failed at first is that of J.K. Rowling, the author of the *Harry Potter* series. She faced innumerable obstacles before tasting success.

'An exceptionally short-lived marriage had imploded, and I was jobless, a lone parent, and as poor as it is possible to be in modern Britain, without being homeless... By every usual standard, I was the biggest failure I knew,' Rowling said during a 2008 Harvard University commencement speech.

Her mother died on New Year's Day in 1991 when Rowling was twenty-five. This was six months after she began writing *Harry Potter*, and she lamented that her mother never knew she was writing it.

Two years later, in 1992, she decided to pick up and move to Portugal for a change of environment, scenery, and a new beginning. It was there that she met a man, married, and gave birth to her daughter. However, it didn't end well for Rowling. In 1993, just one year later, they ended up in a bitter divorce. She decided she needed to head back to the UK, and moved to Edinburgh to be closer to her sister. At the time, she had only completed three chapters of the book, three years after the idea had first come to her mind.

Living in a cramped apartment with her daughter, jobless and penniless, Rowling fell into deep depression and admits she even considered suicide. She was forced to rely on state benefits and spent much of her time writing the book in cafés, with her daughter, Jessica, sleeping in a pram next to her.

She saw herself as a complete failure, someone who had nothing left. And without a hope in the world, she slipped further into depression. With no source of income, she was surviving on government support. It was a dismal time when Rowling couldn't figure out for herself how to come out of the hole that she was in.

But, eventually, she mustered up the fortitude to finish her book. In 1995, she was done. She submitted it to all twelve major publishing houses. And all twelve rejected her. But she persisted and in 1997, a small publishing house called Bloomsbury, at the behest of the owner's daughter, extended an offer to Rowling and the first *Harry Potter* book was published. It had a measly print run of 500 copies, and a very small advance for her that was equivalent to around $2,000. The entire series of seven books has since sold more than 450 million copies, won innumerable awards, been made into movies, and transformed Rowling's life. Rowling is now worth over $1 billion with the *Harry Potter* series estimated at around $15 billion.

Behavioural Signatures That Impede Progress

When things are not going your way, it is all the more important to be focused and keep your motivation levels high so that you give the business a fair chance of getting out of the muck. When the indicators are not looking good, how does it impact the founders and the morale of the employees? Have they taken it as a problem to be solved or have they taken it to mean that the business is on the path of failure? Are there behavioural patterns being exhibited that are not conducive to the revival of the failing business?

Rajiv co-founded a business that provided online booking

of groceries from a local neighbourhood store. It was a hyper-local service based on GPS technology. He thought the sales strategy was faulty and the sales team was not talented enough to close leads. Turnaround time and last mile logistics were not thought through properly. He turned his attention to the online technology platform and said it had far too many bugs and the user interface was shoddy. During the next five minutes, he went through a list of things that were not going right including problems with the other co-founders who were not living up to the expectations. Not once did he take ownership for the failing venture.

Irrespective of the reasons for business failures, one can discern response patterns that make it much more difficult to rise to challenges. You can refer to these response patterns as signatures. These signatures are likely to manifest themselves as responses to the way people interpret events. These can also manifest in organizations that are doing well, in which case, they need to be addressed before they begin to eat at the roots of an organization's emotional health.

Here are some signatures:

- The language of blame and criticism.
- Not taking ownership of actions and shifting responsibility.
- Breakdown of communication.
- Low levels of transparency in disseminating information.
- Increase in gossip and grapevine politics.

Language of Blame and Criticism

Language is a vehicle to express one's thoughts and experiences. When a person gets into the blame mode, it reflects frustration stemming from the way this person has interpreted the world around him. This frustration gets manifested into the language of blame. The language of blame includes both verbal and non-verbal communication. Below are some examples of this language:

- 'He is responsible for the delayed execution.'
- 'Our sales team is good for nothing. They just do not know how to close deals.'
- 'Is this the way things are done here? Schoolchildren can do a better job.'
- 'Customers are terrible, and they do not know what is really good for them.'
- 'You have got the whole strategy wrong. I have been saying this for a long time but nobody listens to me.'
- 'If you do not complete this work by evening, you need not come to the office tomorrow.'

There is constant blaming, threats and search for scapegoats. Some do it with subtle sarcasm, and there are others who can be rude and aggressive. Blame stems from the thought that 'Others are not capable.' When the business is facing challenging times, people start pointing fingers and assume that the reason for the failure lies with others. This attitude does not help the cause of steering the business out of trouble nor does it create a healthy organizational culture. Start-ups are prone to face challenging times, and once the language of blame sets in and persists, it is a sure sign of impending business failure.

Blame expressed using non-verbal body language can be damaging too, such as condescending looks, shrugging of the shoulders, moving the head sideways, sarcastic tone, stamping of the feet and avoiding conversations.

How does one move away from this language of blame? The key is in building emotional intelligence into the fabric of the company. The chapter on EI deals with this topic and provides tools for building EI. This is a skill that can be developed through structured training programmes and follow-up activities.

Ownership

When you start hearing people in leadership positions passing the buck for failures, sooner or later this will translate into a de-motivated workforce, risk averse decision-making, percolation of blame across the organization and lack of momentum, all of which will make the process of getting the organization out of the 'failing' zone even more challenging.

Suresh is a highly energetic, multi-faceted, talented founder of a start-up that provides hands-on science training programs and kits to schools. This required training the teachers, who would, in turn, train the students through hands-on science classes. Marketing collaterals such as brochures and leaflets had to be designed. Suresh had lots of ideas about the content, copy and visual elements that he wished to discuss with his marketing team. He invited ideas from team members, struck down their suggestions and managed to push through his agenda. Since the team was not able to grasp his ideas fully, he decided to design the collaterals all by himself using Adobe Photoshop. He handed over the completed design to the team members, made a few minor changes, and it was ready for distribution. Suresh also made it a point to be present in all the presentations made to clients. In fact, despite having seasoned sales executives in the team, he would insist on making the presentations. Soon after, Suresh realized that it was not possible for him to go to every presentation. He asked his team members to make the next presentation. And they goofed up. An upset Suresh called for a meeting and asked for honest feedback and below is what he received:

- 'I had designed the slides, but Ram gave the presentation.'
- 'You never gave us the opportunity to give presentations on our own earlier.'
- 'I was not comfortable with the content. I thought it would have been better if I had focused on customer benefits rather than the product.'
- 'We did not have sufficient time to practise.'
- 'There were other competitors pitching, and it looked like the customer had already made up his mind about the vendor. He did not show any interest in our presentation.'
- 'The customer was asking irrelevant questions not connected to our solutions.'

Suresh quickly realized his mistake. The issue was less to do with his team. It was more to do with the fact that Suresh had failed to empower his team members to take decisions. *Autonomy* was missing. Suresh did not provide them the opportunities to think, decide and take ownership for their actions. Often, he pushed his agenda because he did not have faith in their abilities and subsequently, *did not allow them to experience failures*. The message that his colleagues received from Suresh was: 'You are not capable.' When the failure happened, people were ready with excuses—blaming others, citing limited time for preparation and looking for excuses. If this attitude gets entrenched, it is likely to de-motivate people and make them dysfunctional at work. Taking ownership for one's actions can be liberating and empowering.

Communication Breakdown

When businesses face challenges, leadership is often confused about what else can be done. There can be a tendency to remain aloof or reclusive. In fact, during hard times, it is even more important to keep the conversations going and have more team meetings. During these times, it is a good idea for the founders to seek guidance from a mentor. Poor eye contact, lack of humour or a smile, being incommunicado and avoiding people, are signs of a breakdown of communication that does not augur well for the business. If you let this continue, it is likely to demoralize people working in the organization.

Lack of Transparency

When the business is not doing well, there is a tendency to withhold information that might be perceived to be detrimental to the interests of the organization. The intention is to ensure that it does not impact the morale of the employees. However, keeping everyone in the dark about everything is likely to contribute to insecurity and ill will among the employees.

ABC, a closely held company, had been facing business-related challenges. Sales growth was not happening, and the net margins were negative for the last six quarters. The company increased its spend on marketing and hired more people to increase sales during the last one year. But the efforts were in vain. People were aware of the 'not so rosy' state of the business through the organization's grapevine, and there were rumours about employee retrenchment. There were no official updates on business performance, and employees were constantly on tenterhooks. The uncertainty and lack of any communication from management raised the stress levels of everyone. People were anxious whenever there was an unscheduled meeting.

Lack of transparency can have serious side effects. It raises the overall stress levels of the organization and undermines goodwill. It also sends the message: 'We do not trust you.' One has to be judicious in the release of information, but a total lack of transparency is undesirable.

Increase in Gossip and Grapevine Politics

It is said that when people meet, there will be politics. And politics goes hand in hand with speculation, gossip and subterfuge. Some gossip is innocuous, but certain other rumours can have a detrimental effect on the morale of the workforce. When the business is not doing well, some begin to see the writing on the wall and are likely to indulge in activities to protect themselves. They are anxious, fearful of losing their job and inadvertently promote rumours about people and the state of the business. This behaviour is related to the lack of transparency. On the other hand, when transparency increases it promotes trust, open communication and a sense of reliability.

Summary

Entrepreneurs go through a tough time when their business venture fails. This chapter focuses on what the entrepreneur is thinking, feeling and doing under these circumstances. Before getting into a logical analysis of the causes of the failure, it is important for the people behind the venture to learn to cope. Strategies and insights have been provided that can help the entrepreneur during these tough times. Resilience is the ability to bounce back from adversity and adapt to rebuild one's life with renewed vigour and energy. Strategies have been provided to help build resilience. We have also looked at the behavioural symptoms that are likely to manifest at the workplace and impede progress.

Coping with business failures is an important skill that every entrepreneur must acquire because entrepreneurship ventures are likely to face many challenging situations that could be overwhelming for the entrepreneur. Learning to recognize behavioural failures will help in addressing potential issues before they become unmanageable.

Acknowledgements

The trigger for writing this book was the positive response I received to my first post on LinkedIn. Many of the ideas shared in this book are based on my observations and thoughts over twenty years of entrepreneurial ventures. My thoughts got refined after being exposed to elements of human behaviour through my wife, Subha, who runs a counselling centre that is focused on parents and children. It is highly unlikely that I would have been able to connect the dots had I not been introduced to many interesting ideas through Subha's workshops on parenting and non-violent communication. I want to thank her for the many wonderful conversations we have had on various aspects of human behaviour that has found its way into this book.

Since this is my first book, I was a complete novice when it came to publishing. I was fortunate to have Mita Kapur as my literary agent. I wish to thank Chris Rowe who helped me edit the first version of the manuscript. He was aligned to my need for keeping the writing style simple and easy to read and it was a pleasure working with him on this project. Special thanks to Tanima Saha, my editor at Rupa, who gave me the first affirmation of the content and style of writing which reinforced my belief in keeping things simple.

I'd also like to thank Elina Majumdar, managing editor at Rupa, for her patience while replying to the queries of a first-time author, and Rudra Sharma, the friendly and energetic commissioning editor and the team at Rupa Publications for placing their faith in my book.

Thank you, Varun and Varsha, my sweet little children, for being patient during the many hours their dad spent in front of a laptop. In fact some of the examples quoted in this book are drawn from my interactions with them.

APPENDIX

Feelings List: When your needs are satisfied[12]

AFFECTIONATE	CONFIDENT	GRATEFUL	PEACEFUL
compassionate	empowered	appreciative	calm
friendly	open	moved	clear-headed
loving	proud	thankful	comfortable
open-hearted	safe	touched	centred
sympathetic	secure	**INSPIRED**	content
tender	**EXCITED**	amazed	equanimous
warm	amazed	awed	fulfilled
ENGAGED	animated	wonder	mellow
absorbed	ardent	**JOYFUL**	quiet
alert	aroused	amused	relaxed
curious	astonished	delighted	relieved
engrossed	dazzled	glad	satisfied
enchanted	eager	happy	serene
entranced	energetic	jubilant	still
fascinated	enthusiastic	pleased	tranquil
interested	giddy	tickled	trusting
intrigued	invigorated	**EXHILARATED**	**REFRESHED**
involved	lively	blissful	enlivened

---

[12]Source: www.cnvc.org

spellbound	passionate	ecstatic	rejuvenated
stimulated	surprised	elated	renewed
HOPEFUL	vibrant	enthralled	rested
expectant		exuberant	restored
encouraged		radiant	revived
optimistic		rapturous	
		thrilled	

Feelings List: When your needs are NOT satisfied[13]

AFRAID	CONFUSED	EMBARRASSED	SAD
apprehensive	ambivalent	ashamed	depressed
dread	baffled	chagrined	dejected
foreboding	bewildered	flustered	despair
frightened	dazed	guilty	disappointed
mistrustful	hesitant	mortified	discouraged
panicked	lost	self-conscious	disheartened
petrified	mystified	**FATIGUE**	forlorn
scared	perplexed	beat	gloomy
suspicious	puzzled	burnt-out	heavy-hearted
terrified	torn	depleted	hopeless
wary	**DISCONNECTED**	exhausted	melancholy
worried	alienated	lethargic	unhappy
ANNOYED	aloof	listless	wretched
aggravated	bored	sleepy	**DISQUIET**
dismayed	cold	tired	agitated
disgruntled	detached	weary	alarmed
displeased	distant	worn out	disconcerted

---

[13]Source: www.cnvc.org

exasperated	distracted	**PAIN**	disturbed
frustrated	indifferent	agony	perturbed
impatient	numb	anguished	rattled
irritated	uninterested	bereaved	restless
irked	withdrawn	devastated	shocked
ANGRY	**AVERSION**	grief	startled
enraged	animosity	heartbroken	surprised
furious	appalled	hurt	troubled
incensed	contempt	lonely	turbulent
indignant	disgusted	miserable	turmoil
irate	dislike	regretful	uncomfortable
livid	hate	remorseful	uneasy
outraged	horrified		unnerved
resentful	hostile		unsettled
	repulsed		upset

List of Needs[14]

SUBSISTENCE AND SECURITY	CONNECTION Affection	MEANING Sense of Self	MEANING Aliveness
Physical	Appreciation	Authenticity	Challenge
Air	Attention	Competence	Consciousness
Food	Closeness	Creativity	Contribution
Health	Companionship	Dignity	Creativity
Movement	Harmony	Growth	Effectiveness
Physical Safety	Intimacy	Healing	Exploration
Rest/Sleep	Love	Honesty	Integration
Water	Nurturing	Integrity	Purpose
Security	Sexual Expression	Self-acceptance	Transcendence

---

[14]Source: www.cnvc.org

Consistency	Support	Self-care	Beauty
Order/Structure	Tenderness	Self-connection	Celebration of life
Peace (external)	Warmth	Self-knowledge	Communion
Peace of mind	**To Matter**	Self-realization	Faith
Protection	Acceptance	Mattering to myself	Flow
Safety (emotional)	Care	**Understanding**	Hope
Stability	Compassion	Awareness	Inspiration
Trusting	Consideration	Clarity	Mourning
FREEDOM	Empathy	Discovery	Peace (internal)
Autonomy	Kindness	Learning	Presence
Choice	Mutual	Making sense of life	**Community**
Ease	Recognition	Stimulation	Belonging
Independence	Respect		Communication
Power	To be heard, seen		Cooperation
Self-responsibility	To be known, understood		Equality
Space	To be trusted		Inclusion
Spontaneity	Understanding others		Mutuality
Leisure			Participation
Humour			Partnership
Joy			Self-expression
Play			Sharing
Pleasure			
Rejuvenation			

Bibliography

Books & Research Papers

1. Stein, Steven J.; Book, Howard E., *Emotional Intelligence and Your Success*, 2006, pp 34–48.
2. Dilts, Robert, *Sleight of Mouth*, 1999, pp 22–56.
3. Dyer, Jeff; Gregerson, Hal; Christensen, Clayton M., *The Innovator's DNA*, 2011, pp 17–25.
4. Christensen, Clayton M.; Raynor, Michael E., *The Innovator's Dilemma*, 2003, pp 32–50.
5. O'Connor, Joseph, *NLP Workbook*, 2001, pp 11–22.
6. The Arbinger Institute, *The Anatomy of Peace*, 2006.
7. The Arbinger Institute, *Leadership and Self-Deception*, 2010, pp 42–49.
8. Rosenberg, Marshall B., *Nonviolent Communication*, 2003, pp 15–22; pp 49–55.
9. Ryan, Richard M.; Deci, Edward L., 'Intrinsic and Extrinsic Motivations: Classic Definitions and New Directions', *Contemporary Educational Psychology*, 25, 2000, pp 54–67.
10. Eccles, Jacquelynne S.; Wigfield, Allan, 'Motivational Beliefs, Values and Goals', *Annual Review of Psychology*, 2002, 53:109–32.
11. Suarez, Fernando; Lanzolla, Gianvito, 'The Half Truth of First Mover Advantage', *Harvard Business Review*, April, 2005.
12. Kantor, Jodi; Streitfeld, David, 'Inside Amazon: Wrestling Big Ideas in a Bruising Workplace', *The New York Times*, 15 August 2015.

13. Hirshberg, Meg Cadoux, 'Why So Many Entrepreneurs Get Divorced', Inc.com, November 2010.
14. Freuler, Jean Marc, 'How to Pick the Right Startup Team', *Forbes*, 23 November 2011.
15. W.K. Kellogg Foundation, 'Intentional Innovation', August 2008.
16. Jones, Andrew, *The Innovation Acid Test: Growth Through Design and Differentiation*, 2008.

Internet

http://www.forbes.com/forbes/2007/0618/154.html
http://greatergood.berkeley.edu/topic/empathy/definition
http://www.6seconds.org/2015/01/02/emotion-feeling-mood/
http://johnvoris.com/featured-articles/difference-between-emotions-and-feelings/
http://www.forbes.com/sites/neilpatel/2015/01/16/90-of-startups-will-fail-heres-what-you-need-to-know-about-the-10/#2715e4857a0bfb35f0055e19
http://www.forbes.com/sites/stevedenning/2011/11/28/maximizing-shareholder-value-the-dumbest-idea-in-the-world/2/#472c75592621
http://www.independent.co.uk/news/business/analysis-and-features/the-moment-it-all-went-wrong-for-kodak-6292212.html
https://en.wikipedia.org/wiki/Kodak
https://en.wikipedia.org/wiki/Macaulay_Culkin
http://www.business2community.com/social-business/5-companies-corporate-social-responsibility-right-0951534#C6UvHe2sS5AFOukT.97
https://en.wikipedia.org/wiki/Evolution_of_corporate_social_responsibility_in_India
http://economictimes.indiatimes.com/news/company/corporate-

trends/mahindra-mahindra-tops-csr-list-in-india-even-as-companies-scale-up-operations/articleshow/49330470.cms

http://principles-of-economics-and-business.blogspot.in/2015/05/why-do-firms-need-growth.html

http://news.bbc.co.uk/2/hi/uk_news/magazine/7674841.stm

http://mashable.com/2013/02/04/why-startups-fail/#0jzevwCBNuq4

http://www.apa.org/helpcentre/road-resilience.aspx

http://celebritytoob.com/reality-tv/10-worst-celebrity-parents-time/

https://www.quora.com/Who-are-some-successful-people-who-failed-at-their-first-try

http://www.businessinsider.in/From-welfare-to-one-of-the-worlds-wealthiest-women-the-incredible-rags-to-riches-story-of-J-K-Rowling/articleshow/47333452.cms